Beacon of Socialism
BHARAT RATNA
Karpoori Thakur

MAMTA MEHROTRA

PRABHAT
PRAKASHAN

Published by
PRABHAT PRAKASHAN PVT. LTD.
4/19 Asaf Ali Road,
New Delhi-110 002 (INDIA)
e-mail: prabhatbooks@gmail.com

ISBN 978-93-5521-963-3

BEACON OF SOCIALISM BHARAT RATNA KARPOORI THAKUR
by Mamta Mehrotra

Edition
First, 2024

Price
₹ 300 (Rupees Three Hundred Only)

Printed at
Japan Art, Delhi

Author's Note

In the political history of Bihar, some personalities emerge not only as leaders, but also, transformative forces who have served to shape the destiny of the state. Jannayak (the people's leader) Karpoori Thakur, who is often referred to as 'common politician' or 'the common man's leader', is indisputably one such great personality. This book, *'Beacon of Socialism: Karpoori Thakur'*, attempts to shed light on his life, political journey and the indelible impact left by him on the socio-political scenario of Bihar and outside it.

As we are setting out in quest of Karpoori Thakur's life, it is impossible to ignore his deep impact on the political ethos of Bihar. Born in an ordinary family in the small village of Pitaunjhia in Samastipur district, the journey of Karpoori Thakur was a symbol of resilience (flexibility), determination and unwavering commitment towards the welfare of the common man. His rise from an ordinary background to the position of chief minister is not only the story of his personal triumph, but also, a reflection of the transformative potential of democratic ideals.

Karpoori Thakur was not only a political figure; he was a person who was deeply connected with the pulse of the common man. This book attempts to capture the essence of his leadership-style, which is distinguished by simplicity, approachability and a deep understanding of the issues that affect the public. Thakur's ability to empathise with the struggles of the average citizen endeared him to the people on a socio-economic level, due to which he gained the title of 'Jannayak' or 'common politician'.

During the Thakur era, Bihar's political scenario was marked with dynamic changes, coalition politics and the inherent challenges of running a state with diverse socio-cultural dynamics. The objective of this book is to provide a comprehensive account of the political journey of Thakur through this complex political arena by carefully delving deep into research and historical records. Every chapter reveals a new aspect of Thakur's political skills from his early political efforts till his tenure as chief minister.

One of the defining characteristics of the political career of Thakur was his unwavering commitment towards social justice. The implementation of reservation policies in government jobs and academic institutions was especially, a historic moment in the history of Bihar. This book carefully examines the circumstances responsible for this unprecedented decision, challenges faced and the lasting legacy of Thakur's advocacy for the marginalised sections of society.

Whereas Thakur is often noted for his initiative of social justice, this book also sheds light on his approach towards economic reforms. His efforts to balance industrial development with social welfare, encourage economic development and modernise agriculture are integral chapters in the story of the economic trajectory of Bihar.

The contribution of Thakur to social justice, especially through the implementation of reservation policies, remains a topic of contemporary relevance. As we explore the legacy of these policies, this book sheds light on its lasting impact on social equality, representation and the ongoing discourse around affirmative action in India.

Thakur's leadership demonstrated his ability as a politician in times of crisis. Whether he had to face dissent within the party, external political opposition or economic challenges, he exhibited a rare mix of flexibility and political skill. This book examines those instances and provides contemporary leaders with lessons through his crisis management skills and experiences.

Whereas, the political journey of Thakur is at the centre of this narrative, the book also examines his contribution beyond the scope of politics. His educational policies, initiatives for agricultural reforms and efforts for the development of the infrastructure contribute to a comprehensive understanding of his multifaceted approach towards administration.

No politician is untouched by controversies and Thakur was no exception to this too. This book confronts those controversies and criticisms that marked his political career and presents a balanced account that considers different viewpoints. By doing so, its objective is to present the detailed picture of a leader who worked in a complex political landscape.

Thakur's commitment to ethical leadership is a thread that runs through this book. As we explore his political strategies, administrative decisions and personal conduct, the narrative underlines the importance of honesty in governance.

This book attempts to provide a glimpse into the personal life of Karpoori Thakur beyond his public persona. His upbringing, family life and the factors that shaped his global perspective provide a deeper understanding of the man behind the leader.

The last few chapters of the book reflect the legacy of Thakur. By analysing the impact of his political thoughts, governance strategies and leadership philosophy, the narrative brings them to the forefront. They are reflected in the form of universal principles not only in the context of Bihar, but also, for ambitious leaders in general.

The life and legacy of Jannayak Karpoori Thakur emerges not only in the form of a 'common politician' as the title suggests, but as evidence of a political philosophy based on service to the common man. This book aspires to be an extensive exploration and to prepare a detailed picture and an insightful reflection on a leader who left an indelible impression on the political canvas of Bihar and continued to inspire generations.

Through the pages of 'Beacon of Socialism: Karpoori Thakur', this journey will be a tribute to a visionary leader, whose legacy is alive not only in the chapters of history, but also, in the hearts of those people who he served. As we bid farewell to the pages of this biography, the essence of Thakur's life echoes - he is a lighthouse for eliminating the complexities of governance politics and for leaders searching for a more fair and just society.

❑

Contents

The Early Days of Karpoori Thakur

Karpoori Thakur, a name that echoes in the political landscape of Bihar, was a charismatic leader and ex-chief minister of the state. The journey of Thakur, born on 24 January 1924, in the small village of Pitaunjhia (now Karpoori Village/Gram) in Samastipur, Bihar, from his humble beginnings to the political corridors of power is the story of resilience, determination and commitment to social justice.

Early life and education

Karpoori Thakur was born in a farmer's family. His father's name was Gokul Thakur and mother's name was Ramdulari Devi. His father was a marginal farmer in the village and practiced his traditional profession as a barber. The young

Karpoori was brought up in a joint family and assimilated the values of simplicity, hard work and a deep sense of community. The socio-economic challenges faced by his family boosted his initial commitment to relieve the worries of marginalised people.

Thakur's educational journey began in a school in the village, where he demonstrated an early ability to learn. However, financial obstacles would often threaten to derail his academic activities. He was fearless and did odd jobs to support his education and demonstrated his determination that became the hallmark of his political career. No one noticed his dedication and he soon became a role model in his village who inspired many youngsters to make efforts for education despite all obstacles.

After completing his primary education, he passed the matriculation examination from Tirhut Academy, Samastipur. Thakur's higher studies were completed from CM College, Darbhanga that was affiliated to Patna University. The bustle of this city was opposite to the peace in his village. He passed the IA examination from here. Thakur's academic journey was marked with an unquenchable thirst for knowledge and he actively participated in various socio-cultural activities, which was a sign of the emergence of a visionary young leader.

Entry into Politics

Karpoori Thakur's entry into politics was not predetermined, rather it was a response to the burning socio-political issues of his time. The era after independence was marked with a wave of social and economic changes and Thakur found himself attracted to a political journey, whose objective was to address the needs of the marginalised sections of society.

His political career formally began with his participation in the 'Quit India Movement' in the early 1940s. His participation in the revolution displayed his commitment to the independence of India and his courage to challenge colonial officers. This early display of political activism laid the foundation of his future as the champion of social justice.

After being associated with the socialist movement in Bihar, Thakur's political journey continued to advance. He was inspired by the ideology of leaders like Jayaprakash Narayan and actively participated in agitations advocating land reforms and social equality. His magnetic personality and ability to connect with people at the grassroots level soon gave him recognition in socialist circles.

Grassroots Leader

The rise of Karpoori Thakur in the politics of Bihar was inspired not from the traditional power structure; rather, it was inspired from his connection to the grassroots level and genuine concern for the welfare of the common man. He made unrelenting efforts to solve the problems of farmers, labourers and the underprivileged. Thakur's deep understanding of the agricultural crisis in Bihar and ability to articulate public grievances made him a prominent figure in the political scenario.

In the year 1952, Thakur was elected as a member of the Bihar Legislative Assembly (MLA) for the first time, representing the Socialist Party and thus began his long and influential legislative career. He continued to support social justice and actively participated in debates and discussions with the aim of the upliftment of the marginalised sections of society.

Thakur had an unrelenting commitment towards socialist ideology. He played an important role in the coalition of socialist parties and the formation of the joint legislative party which emerged as a powerful force in the politics of Bihar. His leadership skills and ability to form alliances significantly contributed to the success of the alliance in Bihar Legislative Assembly elections in 1967.

Tenure as Chief Minister

He became the chief minister of Bihar for the first time on 22 December 1970 and remained in this position for about five months. He became the chief minister once again on 24 June 1977 and remained in office till 21 April 1979.

With the end of the Emergency in 1977 and return of democratic governance, the politics of India took a historic turn. In this duration, Karpoori Thakur took over as chief minister of Bihar as the leader of the Janata Party government. This was a decisive moment in Thakur's political career and he assumed the responsibilities of chief minister with the view of overall development.

As chief minister, Thakur implemented many progressive measures with the aim to eliminate socio-economic disparities in the state. One of his notable initiatives was his decision to implement the '20-point socio-economic programme' which was focused on land reforms, employment creation and education. This step shows his commitment to convert socialist principles into tangible policies for the welfare of the people.

Many bold decisions were taken during his tenure as chief minister that also included the abolition of the zamindari system, the objective of which was to redistribute land to the landless. This step was appreciated as a revolutionary step in the direction of agricultural reforms and he was praised for his commitment towards social justice. Moreover, by giving importance to education and health services as fundamental rights, his government worked to bring about an improvement in the circumstances of the marginalised communities.

Challenges and Criticisms

Even though Karpoori Thakur's tenure as chief minister was marked by many progressive initiatives, it was not without challenges and criticisms. During this period, the political scenario was complex and the newly formed Janata Party was struggling with internal dissent. Thakur had to face criticism from various quarters that also included sections within his own party.

One of the controversial decisions during his tenure was the implementation of the reservation policy for the economically backward classes (EBC). This step which was taken with the aim of providing reservation to the economically deprived sections had to face opposition and criticism from various quarters. However, Thakur defended his decision and argued that this was an important step in the direction of ensuring equal opportunities for all sections of society.

Legacy and Impact

Karpoori Thakur's legacy extends even beyond his tenure as chief minister. His impact on the political landscape of Bihar is indelible and his contribution to social justice and agricultural reforms continues to shape discussions on overall governance. Although the 20-point programme was facing challenges, it laid the foundation of his later initiative that aimed to eliminate socio-economic disparities in the state.

Thakur's emphasis on education as an instrument of empowerment echoed in his own journey from a small village to the political corridors of power. The educational reforms started during his tenure prepared the stage for reforms in the education system of the state. His focus on primary education and efforts to reduce the school drop-out rate reflected his perspective of building a socially and economically empowered Bihar.

After his tenure as chief minister, Karpoori Thakur continued to remain an influential figure in the politics of Bihar. He remained committed to the socialist ideology and actively participated in various agitations that advocated for the rights of the marginalised people. His leadership and commitment to social justice earned him the nickname of 'Jannayak' or People's Leader among his supporters.

A Visionary Politician: The Early Years of Karpoori Thakur

Karpoori Thakur's journey from the peaceful village of Pitaunjhia to the bustling political corridors was marked by the confluence of transformative influences that shaped his vision and established him at the centre of the socio-political landscape of Bihar. This chapter sheds light on the early years of this leader and explores those influences, struggles and significant moments that defined the emergence of Karpoori Thakur as a visionary leader.

Early Influences and Ideological Foundation

Thakur's early years were deeply influenced by the socio-economic fabric of rural Bihar. Brought up in a joint family of farmers, he witnessed firsthand, the struggles and aspirations of the farming community. The acute disparities prevalent in the agricultural society left an indelible impression on the young Thakur, which sowed the seeds of his commitment to eliminate the socio-economic disparities prevalent in his community.

After independence, the socialist ideologies taking root in India found fertile ground in his mind. The ideas propagated by leaders such as Jayaprakash Narayan matched his own observations about the rural crisis and economic inequality. Thakur quickly joined those discussions and activities which were focussed on the principles of socialism, advocacy for land reforms, equitable distribution of resources and social justice.

During the 1940s, Thakur's initial performance in the 'Quit India Movement' further boosted his political consciousness. This movement that was launched with the aim of ousting the British colonial rulers from power, created group spirit and this confidence in him that collective action can bring about transformative changes. These early influences prepared the groundwork for the later efforts of Thakur as the champion of the marginalised people.

Educational Objective: The Path of Empowerment

Karpoori Thakur's search for education was not only a personal effort, rather, it was a conscious choice to break the shackles of rural poverty and empower himself with the tools of knowledge. His journey from the village school at Pitaunjhia to the classrooms of Darbhanga College was marked by financial difficulties and a continuous quest for academic excellence.

While facing economic obstacles, Thakur did odd jobs to support his education and displayed a remarkable determination that became symbolic of his later political career. His academic talent was helped by active participation in socio-cultural activities, where he honed his oratory skills and developed a deep understanding of the issues troubling society.

Thakur's education not only broadened his intellectual horizons, but also, created a feeling of responsibility towards the larger community in him. As soon as he delved deeply into subjects such as political science and sociology, he began to associate the theoretical framework with the experiences of the people around him. This intellectual synthesis laid the foundation for his future role as a thoughtful leader and policy architect.

Early Political Consciousness

After independence, the political landscape of Bihar provided fertile ground for the germination of Thakur's political aspirations. His early entry in active politics was through his participation in the 'Quit India Movement', where he worked shoulder to shoulder with like-minded people who shared his passion for social change. Thakur's early activism was characterised by his fearlessness to challenge the status quo and unrelenting commitment towards independence as well as the principles of equality.

The socialist movement, which gathered speed in the 1950s, became the rallying point of his political activism. This movement which laid emphasis on social justice, egalitarianism and land reforms, was deeply in line with his own beliefs. Thakur actively participated in grassroots level movements to alleviate the concerns of farmers and labourers, through which, he was recognised as an emerging star in socialist circles.

His ability to articulate the grievances of marginalised people and charismatic leadership style gave him a different identity immediately. Thakur's entry into electoral politics was the natural progression of his activism at the grassroots level. In 1952, he was elected as a legislator for the first time, representing the Socialist Party. This was the beginning of his legislative career where he shaped policies and advocated the rights of the common man.

Joint Legislative Party: Forming an Alliance

With the emergence of coalition politics in the 1960s, there was a significant change in the political landscape of Bihar. Karpoori Thakur played an important role through his efforts in forming alliances and bringing together like-minded parties under the banner of the Samyukta Vidhayak Dal (united legislative party).

Thakur's ability to bridge ideological differences and form an alliance of socialist parties was proof of his political skills. The Samyukta Vidhayak Dal (united legislative party), formed in 1967, emerged as a powerful force in the politics of Bihar that challenged the supremacy of established political institutions. Thakur's leadership skills and commitment towards a common socio-political agenda played an important role in the success of the alliance in the Assembly elections.

This period proved to be a turning point in Thakur's political career because he became a prominent player in the political landscape of the state from a grassroots level leader. The victory of the alliance in the elections established Thakur as a leader who had the ability to bring about a tangible change in Bihar.

Karpoori's Journey from Village to Politics

Karpoori's journey from the rural simplicity of Pitaunjhia to the dynamic realm of politics is a story that connects the personal to the political. The outline of Thakur's political identity was formed by his grassroots activism, where he immersed himself in the struggles of the common man. The agricultural crisis in Bihar, which was characterised by pertinent issues such as tenant disputes, inequitable distribution of land and exploitation of labourers, became the focus of his advocacy. Thakur emerged as a prominent voice for the marginalised people through movements and his participation in them.

His ability to connect with the public at the grassroots level establishes him as a leader who understood the pulse of the people. Thakur's charisma, combined with his genuine concern for the welfare of the common man, earned him the trust and admiration of those people who he wanted to represent. Thakur's early years in politics were marked by his commitment towards social justice, whether it be addressing the concerns of farmers or advocating the rights of labourers.

His rise to the position of chief minister was the symbol of the realisation of a dream cherished in Pitaunjhia village and of the journey from the grassroots level to the peak of political power. Thakur's tenure as chief minister was one of a visionary approach to governance.

The challenges that Thakur had to face during the period of his chief ministership underlined the complexities of governance, especially in a diverse and socio-economically stratified state like Bihar. A delicate balance was required to deal with the complex web of political gains, social dynamism and economic disparities and Thakur's response to these challenges reflects his commitment to principled governance.

One of the lasting legacies of the period of Thakur's chief ministership was his emphasis on education as an instrument of empowerment. The initiative taken for improvement in the education system of the state reflects his belief that education is the key to break the shackles of poverty and inequality. His efforts to focus on primary education and reduce the school dropout rate symbolised his perspective of a socially and economically strong Bihar.

His journey from a village to the political sphere not only includes the story of a person, but also reflects the collective aspirations and struggles of those people who he served.

❑

The Political Landscape of Bihar: Karpoori's Entry

In the mid-20th century, the political landscape of Bihar was marked by a confluence of social, economic and political turmoil. The socio-political canvas of Bihar, with its diverse challenges and opportunities, shaped the path of Thakur's political journey.

In the 1950s and 1960s, important changes were seen in the socio-political structure of Bihar. The predominantly agricultural state was struggling with issues such as land reform, caste-based disparities and economic imbalance. The dominance of feudal structures and the deeply rooted zamindari system contributed to the unbalanced distribution of resources, due to which, socio-economic disparities increased.

The seeds of dissatisfaction were sown in the fertile fields of Bihar, which gave rise to various socio-political movements. The agricultural crisis combined with the search for social justice and provided fertile ground for socialist movements to take root. Leaders such as Jayaprakash Narayan were helpful in inspiring people, expressing their concerns and advocating revolutionary changes.

The Rise of Socialist Movements

Karpoori Thakur's entry into politics coincided with the growing influence of the socialist ideology in Bihar. The socialist revolution that emphasised on land reforms, social equality and the upliftment of Dalits found resonance among the deprived masses. Thakur's early involvement in the Quit India Movement and later, his participation in socialist circles, established him as a proponent of change in the emerging political landscape.

The Samyukta Samajwadi Dal became a precedent for the expression of socialist principles under the leadership of leaders such as Ram Manohar Lohia and Jayaprakash Narayan. Through his grassroots activism and legislative efforts, Thakur became an integral part of this movement. The socialist ideology provided ethical guidelines (moral compass) to solve the complexities of the political circles of Bihar and guide Thakur's work and policies.

Electoral Landscape and Political Alliance

With the arrival of coalition politics in the 1960s, Bihar's electoral landscape was going through a period of change. Traditional political structures were being challenged and new alliances were being formed to face established centres of power. Thakur's role in the formation of the Samyukta Vidhayak Dal presented an example of the changing dynamics of Bihar's political landscape.

The Samyukta Vidhayak Dal was an alliance of socialist parties, which included the Samyukta Socialist Party, the Praja Socialist Party and other parties. The formation of this alliance was in response to the need for a united front against the prevailing political system. Thakur's skill in forming the alliances and promoting unity between ideologically diverse parties marked him as a strategic architect in the political sphere.

Electoral Success and Legislative Impact

The assembly elections of 1967 proved to be an important turning point in the path of the political trajectory of Bihar. The Samyukta Vidhayak Dal secured an important mandate in the important role of Thakur. On 5 March 1967, Thakur was appointed Deputy Chief Minister as well as the finance and education minister in the Mahamaya Prasad Sinha cabinet. As the education minister, Thakur took the bold decision to abolish the compulsory subject of English in the matriculation examination.

Under Thakur's leadership, the government worked towards bringing about improvements in the educational infrastructure and ensuring the access to quality education for children throughout the state. The emphasis on primary education was a strategic step to lay the foundation of a more literate and informed populace for the socio-economic development of Bihar, in line with Thakur's comprehensive vision.

He remained in office till 28 January 1968.

The victory of the coalition was a symbol of deviation from traditional power structures and Thakur was established as a leader who had the ability to bring about a significant change. Thakur's impact in the legislative sphere was immediate and profound. As an elected representative, he continued to advocate for the interests of marginalised people and actively participated in debates and discussions that shaped legislative agendas. His early years in the Legislative Assembly demonstrated his commitment to the principles of social justice and consistent adherence to policies aimed towards the socio-economic upliftment of the deprived.

His entry into politics was not an isolated act, rather, it was the response of the collective aspiration of a changing society.

❑

The Political Rise of Karpoori Thakur

The political rise of Karpoori Thakur from the grassroots level to the peak of power is proof of his indomitable spirit, political skills and tireless commitment to the welfare of the common man. Thakur's early years in politics had been defined by his grassroots level activism and strong commitment to the interests of marginalised people. His entry into electoral politics marked a natural progression as he tried to translate his advocacy into legislative action. In 1952, he was elected as a member of the Legislative Assembly (MLA) for the first time, representing the Socialist Party.

As a legislator, Thakur demonstrated his legislative power by actively participating in debates and discussions. His speeches had a deep understanding of the socio-economic challenges facing the people of Bihar. Thakur's legislative initiatives were focussed on issues like land reforms, labour rights and social justice that were preparing the basis of his later political trajectory.

Formation of the Samyukta Vidhayak Dal

With the emergence of coalition politics in the 1960s, a model change was observed in the political landscape of Bihar. Karpoori Thakur played an important role in this through his efforts in the formation of the Samyukta Vidhayak Dal in 1967. This alliance, in which various socialist parties were included, became a strong force that challenged the supremacy of established political institutions.

Thakur's ability to form an alliance and unify ideologically diverse parties demonstrated his strategic skills . The formation of the Samyukta Vidhayak Dal was a significant moment in the political history of Bihar, which ushered in a new era of cooperative governance. Within the alliance, Thakur's leadership prepared the stage for his future role as a consensus builder and unifying force in the politics of the state.

Ministerial Roles and Administrative Influence

Thakur's rise in the political hierarchy gained momentum with his appointment to a ministerial post in the state government. His first ministerial assignment came in 1967 when he became the finance and education minister of Bihar. During this, his administrative skills and proactive approach earned praise, through which, he gained recognition as a leader capable of converting socialist principles into tangible governance. Thakur's impact on land reforms prepared the stage for more comprehensive roles in the coming years.

A Visionary Leader

Thakur's peak of political progress came with his appointment as chief minister of Bihar in 1977. The victory of the Janata Party after the Emergency, paved the way for Thakur to assume the highest political office in the state. His tenure from 1977 to 1979 was marked by a visionary approach to governance because he had tried to address the long-standing socio-economic issues of Bihar.

During his tenure as chief minister, one of Thakur's historic initiatives was the implementation of the '20-point socio-economic programme'. This comprehensive policy framework touched key areas such as land reforms, employment creation, education and health care. This programme was the manifestation of Thakur's commitment to overall development, which set an example for future governments in the state.

Land Reforms: Breaking Feudal Shackles

One of the cornerstones of Thakur's agenda as chief minister was the abolition of the zamindari system and the implementation of land reforms. The feudal structure that perpetuated social and economic disparities was a long-standing obstacle for progress in Bihar. The objective of Thakur's bold decision to abolish this system was to redistribute land to the landless and break the shackles of feudal dominance.

The implementation of land reforms under Thakur's leadership was a transformational moment in the agricultural landscape of Bihar. It made efforts to empower those people who were historically marginalised. They were provided with the means to break free from the cycle of poverty and exploitation. Thakur's strong commitment to social justice found tangible expression in this important policy decision.

20-point Programme: A Comprehensive Approach

Thakur's tenure as chief minister was marked by the ambitious implementation of the 20-point socio-economic programme. This comprehensive policy initiative addressed many issues reflecting Thakur's multifaceted approach to governance. This programme was not merely a set of policy formulae , but a visionary blueprint for the overall development of Bihar.

Land Reforms

Thakur's commitment to land reforms was reiterated and expanded in the programme. Its objective was to make land available to the landless, break the chains of feudalism and introduce a more equitable (fair) agrarian structure. The focus on land redistribution was the affirmation of Thakur's faith in the transformative power of providing access to marginalised people to the same resources that have historically been the symbol of power and privilege.

Employment Generation

Recognising the importance of employment for socio-economic upliftment, the programme outlined measures to generate employment opportunities. Thakur envisioned a Bihar where every citizen would have the means to free himself from the clutches of poverty and earn a livelihood. The emphasis on employment generation reflects his commitment to empower individuals and communities through economic self-reliance.

Education

Education emerged as the cornerstone of Thakur's vision for a progressive Bihar. The 20-point programme underlined the need for educational reforms with focus on primary education and efforts to reduce the school dropout rate. Thakur recognized education as a catalyst for social and economic empowerment, which laid thc foundation for a more literate and informed populace.

Healthcare

The programme also addressed health care, acknowledging the importance of a healthy population in the overall development of the state. The outline of an initiative was prepared to improve the infrastructure of health services and access to them, which reflects Thakur's holistic approach to governance. The emphasis on healthcare was in line with his broader vision of building a society where welfare was not a luxury but a fundamental right.

The 20-point programme, with its holistic and inclusive vision, became a touchstone for subsequent policies in Bihar. Thakur's ability to envision a comprehensive roadmap for the development of the state reflects his leadership skills and his determination to address the root causes of socio-economic disparities.

Challenges and Controversies

Thakur's tenure as chief minister was not without challenges and controversies. The implementation of the EBC reservation policy gave rise to debate and opposition. Critics argued that this policy could potentially reduce the benefits of reservation for socially marginalised groups. However, Thakur defended his decision by stressing the need for equal opportunities for all sections of the society.

The controversy surrounding the EBC reservation policy highlighted the need for a complex balancing act to deal with the complex socio-political scenario. During this period, Thakur's flexibility underlined his commitment to those policies whose objective was the overall development of the state, despite opposition and criticism.

❑

Karpoori's Growing Influence

As Karpoori Thakur's political journey advanced, his influence grew beyond regional boundaries, making him a prominent leader at the national level. From his contribution to national movements to his role in shaping political discourse, Thakur emerged as a leader among his peers and left an indelible mark on the socio-political landscape of India.

National Relevance: Thakur's Role in the Janata Party

The post-Emergency period in Indian politics was marked by demands for change and the revival of democratic principles. The Janata Party - a coalition of opposition parties - emerged as the torchbearer of this democratic revival. Karpoori Thakur played an important role in the Janata Party, contributed to its ideology and participated in its leadership.

Thakur's association with the Janata Party reflects his commitment to a comprehensive national agenda. His credibility (authenticity) as a leader dedicated to social justice and inclusive governance made him a unifying force within the diverse alliance. As the party prepared for the 1977 general elections, Thakur's presence lent authenticity to the Janata Party's commitment to democratic values and people-centred governance.

National Recognition: Ministry of Railways

Thakur's leadership qualities attracted national attention after the Janata Party's victory in the general elections of March 1977. In this general election, Karpoori Thakur was elected to the Lok Sabha for the first time as a Janata Party candidate from Samastipur Lok Sabha constituency by defeating Yamuna Prasad Mandal of Congress (I) by a total of 3,27,434 votes, but in the same year, only three months later in June, he was made the chief minister of Bihar for the second time.

Thakur's influence extended beyond administrative roles. His commitment to social justice and dedication to the upliftment of marginalised people found expression in various initiatives beyond the borders of Bihar. Thakur actively participated in national movements and campaigns with the aim of eliminating socio-economic inequalities and advocating the rights of the underprivileged.

In the year 1978, he made provision for reservation for backward castes, women and the poor. Under this, 8 percent reservation was made for backward, 12 percent for extremely backward, 3 percent for women and 3 percent for economically backward upper castes. Thakur's insight into the challenges faced by these communities was instrumental in formulating policies that aimed to reduce disparities and ensure equal opportunities.

Advocacy for Social Justice

Thakur's advocacy for social justice went beyond bureaucratic responsibilities. He continued to remain actively associated with various forums and movements that advocated for the interests of the marginalised people. His speeches, writings and participation in national debates reflect a deep understanding of the socio-political challenges facing India. As a staunch supporter of the rights of Dalits, Thakur's voice echoed not only in Bihar but throughout the country.

Political Dynamism and Challenges

While Thakur's national roles brought him recognition, they also made him aware of the complex dynamism of coalition politics at the national level. The Janata Party, a group of diverse political ideologies, had to face internal challenges, which ultimately led to its split. The complexities of managing a coalition of differing interests and ideologies presented challenges that required skilful political manoeuvring.

Thakur's ability to deal with these challenges, maintain his principled stance and the interests of the common man demonstrated his flexibility and political astuteness. Despite internal rifts within the Janata Party, Thakur's commitment to the values of social justice and inclusive governance remained unwavering.

Advocacy for the Marginalised: An Ongoing Commitment

Thakur's advocacy for the rights of marginalised people remained the central theme of his political agenda. At the state or national level, he remained committed to eliminating the socio-economic inequalities plaguing Indian society. Thakur's efforts were not limited only to policy initiatives; he also actively participated in movements and initiatives with the aim of creating awareness about the challenges faced by the underprivileged.

Reservation Policies

Thakur's advocacy for reservation policies for socially and economically backward classes remained steadfast. He continued to emphasise the need for affirmative action to ensure equal opportunities and representation for marginalised communities. Thakur's stance on reservation policies reflects his commitment to build a more inclusive and just society. Thakur's ability to seamlessly transition between state and national roles reflected his versatility and enduring relevance in the political sphere.

❑

The Ideals of Karpoori Thakur

Karpoori Thakur's political journey was based on the principles of social justice. Thakur's unwavering commitment to the upliftment of the marginalised, elimination of social inequalities and advocacy for the underprivileged established him as a true champion of social justice.

Roots in Socialism

Thakur's political journey began in the backdrop of the socialist movement in post-independence India. Influenced by leaders such as Ram Manohar Lohia and Jayaprakash Narayan, Thakur's early exposure to socialist ideologies laid the foundation for his commitment to social justice. The principles of socialism, focusing on equitable distribution of resources and opportunities, became the guiding principles of Thakur's political career.

Land Reforms: Addressing Economic Inequalities

One of the fundamental pillars of Thakur's social justice agenda was land reforms. Bihar's agrarian landscape was characterised by feudal structures, which perpetuated economic inequalities. As MLA and later, as Chief Minister, Thakur initiated the abolition of the zamindari system and redistributed land to the landless. The objective of this transformative policy was to break the chains of feudal dominance and empower the economically marginalised people.

The impact of land reforms went far beyond mere economic redistribution. This was a strategic move to provide economic support to the historically disenfranchised people. Thakur's commitment to remove economic inequalities through land reforms reflects his deep understanding of the interrelationship between economic and social justice.

Advocacy for Labour Rights

Thakur's socialist ideals extended to workers' rights. He actively advocated for the interests of workers, advocating for fair wages, better working conditions and protection of labour rights. Thakur's involvement in labour movements and his legislative efforts demonstrate his commitment to create an environment where the working class can assert its rights and claim a fair share in the economic holding.

The interrelationship of Thakur's social justice ideals to address the multi-dimensional challenges faced by different sections of the society was evident in his holistic approach. From agricultural reforms to labour rights, he envisioned a society where economic opportunities would be accessible to all, regardless of their social or economic background.

The Gateway to Social Justice

Thakur recognised education as a powerful tool for social change. His advocacy for educational empowerment was based on the belief that access to quality education can break the cycle of poverty and uplift communities. Thakur's initiative in the field of education was to ensure that every child would have the opportunity to receive a meaningful education regardless of his socio-economic background.

Priority to Primary Education

As chief minister, Thakur prioritised primary education as the cornerstone of his social justice agenda. Recognising that the foundation of a just society lay in an educated population, he directed efforts at improving the primary education infrastructure. Emphasising the early years of education was a strategic move to lay the foundation for a literate and informed citizenry.

Reducing Dropout Rates

Thakur's commitment towards educational empowerment extended to addressing the issue of high dropout rates, especially among marginalised communities. He implemented measures to create a favourable environment for continuous educational activities, recognising that reducing dropout rates was important to ensure that the benefits of education reach the intended beneficiaries.

Empowering Women

Thakur's social justice agenda was inclusive and included the empowerment of women through education. He believed that educating women was not only a matter of individual rights, but also, a catalyst for social progress. Thakur's initiative, aimed at increasing educational opportunities for girls, reflects his commitment to eliminating gender-based barriers to education.

Inclusive Governance

An important aspect of Thakur's social justice agenda was the implementation of reservation policies. Recognising the historical injustice resulting from caste-based discrimination, he supported affirmative action to ensure representation and opportunities for marginalised communities.

Economically Backward Class (EBC) Reservation

Thakur's decision to implement reservation policies for economically backward classes (EBC) had to face challenges and controversies. Critics argued that this policy could reduce the benefits of reservation for socially marginalised groups. However, Thakur defended his decision by stressing the need for equal opportunities for all sections of the society, regardless of caste or class.

The controversy associated with EBC reservation underlined the complexities of navigating the socio-political landscape to achieve a balance between the interests of different groups. Thakur's stance reflects his commitment to a nuanced approach to social justice that considers the interrelated factors of caste and economic status.

Scheduled Caste (SC) and Scheduled Tribe (ST) Reservation

Thakur's commitment to reservation policies extended to the Scheduled Castes (SC) and Scheduled Tribes (ST). He recognised the historical injustices suffered by these communities and advocated for policies that would provide them access to opportunities in education, employment and governance.

The implementation of reservation policies was not merely a symbolic gesture for Thakur; it was a concrete step towards dismantling centuries-old structures of discrimination and creating a more inclusive society.

Economic Reforms: Bridging the Socio-economic gap

Thakur's perspective of social justice included addressing the economic inequalities affecting Bihar. The objective of his economic reforms was to create an environment where prosperity was not limited to a few, but spread across the entire socio-economic spectrum.

Abolition of the Zamindari System

The abolition of the zamindari system was a historic economic reform which had a deep social impact. By dismantling this feudal structure, Thakur aimed to redistribute land to the landless, thus breaking the stranglehold of economic inequality perpetuated by centuries-old systems.

The economic impact of this reform was two-fold—it empowered those who were historically marginalised and laid the foundation for a more equitable distribution of resources. Thakur's commitment to economic justice was expressed in this transformative policy decision.

Employment Generation

Recognising the importance of employment in socio-economic upliftment, Thakur's policies included measures to create employment opportunities. His vision was to create an environment where every citizen would have the means to earn a livelihood, free from the clutches of poverty.

The emphasis on job creation reflects Thakur's understanding of the symbiotic relationship between economic opportunities and social justice. Creating avenues of employment was a strategic move to empower individuals and communities through economic self-reliance.

The Legacy of Social Justice: Beyond Policies

Thakur's legacy as a champion of social justice goes far beyond the policies that he implemented. This is inherent in the ethos of his leadership, the principles that he adopted and his lasting impact on the socio-political fabric of Bihar. His vision for a just and equitable society was not limited only to his tenure as chief minister; it also became a guiding light for future leaders and policy-makers.

The Leader of the Common Man: Jannayak

The title of 'Jannayak' (People's Leader) was not merely an honour (honorific) for Thakur; it encapsulated the essence of his leadership. His ability to connect with the masses, prioritise their needs and advocate for their interests cemented his place as a leader who stood with and for the people.

Thakur's advocacy for social justice was not separate from the realities of the common man. He spoke the language of the marginalised people, understood their struggles and fought for a society where their rights were not only accepted, but also, actively protected.

Commitment to Inclusive Governance

Thakur's commitment to social justice was not a one-dimensional approach; it permeated every aspect of governance. His emphasis on inclusive policies, representation for all sections of society and creation of opportunities for the underprivileged reflects a comprehensive vision of social justice that goes beyond symbolism.

The principles of inclusive governance propounded by Thakur became a standard for subsequent administration in Bihar. His legacy influenced the framework of governance and shaped policies aimed at bridging the socio-economic gap and ensuring a more just social order.

Lasting Impact on the Political Scenario of Bihar

Thakur's ideals of social justice left a lasting impact on the political landscape of Bihar. The discourse changed and subsequent leaders found themselves held to the standards set by the 'Jannayak'. The principles of social justice became an integral part of the political narrative and Thakur's legacy continued to shape the aspirations and expectations of the people.

❑

Chief Minister: Karpoori's First Term

Karpoori Thakur assumed the office of chief minister on 22 June 1970 and this was an important turning point in the political scenario of Bihar. His commitment to social justice and economic development laid the foundation for a transformative era in the history of the state. However, his tenure lasted only for about five months till 2 June 1971.

Social Justice Reforms

Karpoori Thakur, who was known for his staunch advocacy for social justice, introduced important reforms aimed at the upliftment of the marginalised sections of the society. One of his landmark decisions was to implement reservation policy in government jobs and educational institutions. The move was aimed at providing opportunities for Scheduled Castes, Scheduled Tribes and Other Backward Classes, so that inclusiveness could be promoted and historically oppressed communities could be empowered.

Under Thakur's leadership, Bihar saw the formulation and implementation of policies that addressed the socio-economic inequalities prevalent in the state. He was committed to creating an egalitarian society, where every citizen would have access to opportunities, regardless of his or her caste or social background.

Educational Revolution

Recognizing the important role of education in shaping a progressive society, Karpoori Thakur launched several initiatives to reform the education system of the state. His government made significant investments in the establishment and improvement of schools and colleges, especially in rural areas. Emphasis was laid on providing quality education to children of all sections of the society.

Innovative educational programmes, scholarships and schemes of financial assistance were introduced during Thakur's tenure to ensure that every child, irrespective of his economic background, could access education without any barrier. This commitment to education laid the foundation for a more literate and informed Bihar.

Economic Development and Agricultural Reforms

Karpoori Thakur recognised the importance of agricultural development in the overall progress of Bihar. His government introduced comprehensive agricultural reforms aimed at increasing productivity and improving the socio-economic status of farmers. Initiatives such as irrigation projects, agricultural extension services and provision of subsidies on seeds and fertilizers contributed to significant reforms in the agricultural sector.

Thakur's administration also prioritised the development of small and medium-sized industries to create employment opportunities and stimulate economic development. His visionary economic policies were aimed at diversifying Bihar's economy and reducing the dependence on agriculture as well as promoting a more resilient and sustainable development model.

Infrastructure Development

Infrastructure development emerged as a major focus area during the first term of Karpoori Thakur. His government invested in the building and improvement of roads, bridges and other essential infrastructure projects. This not only provided better connectivity within the state, but also, laid the groundwork for attracting investment and promoting trade and commerce.

Thakur's commitment to infrastructure development extended to the healthcare and sanitation sectors. The purpose of establishing hospitals, health centres and sanitation programmes was to improve public health and create an environment conducive to the overall well-being of the citizens.

Empowerment of Women

Karpoori Thakur recognised the importance of women empowerment in building a progressive society. His government took important steps to address the challenges faced by women in Bihar. In order to enhance the socio-economic status of women in the state, initiatives such as women's education programmes, skill development initiatives and promotion of women's participation in local governance structures were introduced.

Thakur's tenure saw the implementation of policies and laws aimed at ensuring the safety and welfare of women. His commitment to gender equality set the stage for a more inclusive and empowered society.

In conclusion, Karpoori Thakur's first tenure as the chief minister of Bihar was characterised by visionary leadership, commitment to social justice and a holistic approach to development. The achievements and initiatives during this period laid the foundation for Bihar's progress in the years to come. Thakur's legacy as a champion of the marginalised people and a visionary leader will continue to inspire future generations, making his tenure an important chapter in the history of Bihar.

❑

Chief Minister: Karpoori's Second Term

As soon as Karpoori Thakur assumed office as chief minister for the second time on 24 June 1977, Bihar was eagerly anticipating a continuation of the transformational leadership that had characterised his first term. This tenure also lasted for almost two years till 21 April 1979.

Integrating Social Justice Reforms

Building on the foundation laid in his first term, Karpoori Thakur remained committed to social justice. In his second term, the reservation policy was strengthened, its effective implementation was ensured and any flaws that arose were removed. Focusing on creating a more equitable (fair) and inclusive society, Thakur's government also took measures to monitor and evaluate the impact of these policies.

In addition to reservation policies, Thakur's administration introduced innovative affirmative action programmes aimed at empowering marginalised communities. These initiatives included skill development programmes, access to entrepreneurship opportunities and credit facilities, promotion of economic independence and social mobility etc.

Education for All

Education remained a priority for Karpoori Thakur during his second term. Recognising the vital role of education in shaping the future of the state, his government implemented comprehensive measures to raise the quality of education and expand its reach.

Thakur's second term saw the establishment of new schools and colleges, especially in remote and deprived areas. The focus became not only on increasing enrolment, but also, on improving the standard of education through teacher training programmes and curriculum reforms. The goal was to create a strong education system that would equip the youth with the skills needed for a rapidly evolving world.

Agricultural Progress and Rural Development

Karpoori Thakur's commitment towards the agriculture sector continued in his second term. Recognising the challenges faced by farmers, his government implemented policies to increase agricultural productivity, promote sustainable farming practices and ensure fair prices for agricultural produce.

Innovative measures such as the introduction of technology in agriculture, support for organic farming and establishment of farmer cooperative societies were aimed at empowering farmers and making agriculture a more attractive business. Thakur's emphasis on rural development went beyond agriculture to include initiatives related to rural infrastructure, electrification and access to clean drinking water.

Infrastructure for Progress

The second term of Karpoori Thakur saw significant growth in infrastructure development. Recognising the importance of a well-connected state for economic development, his government invested in the expansion and maintenance of roads, bridges and transportation networks. These efforts not only facilitated better connectivity within Bihar, but also established the state as an attractive destination for investment.

Along with establishing modern facilities and promoting sustainable urban planning, Thakur's administration also focused on urban development. The development of industrial areas and creation of employment opportunities in urban areas were aimed at addressing the challenges of rural-urban migration and promoting balanced regional development.

Empowering Women and Minorities

Karpoori Thakur's commitment towards the empowerment of women and minorities remained unwavering even in his second term. His government introduced targeted programmes to address the specific challenges facing these groups, including access to education, healthcare and economic opportunities.

Thakur's policies included awareness campaigns, legal reforms and the building of support systems aimed at promoting gender equality and minority rights. The focus was not only on eliminating existing inequalities, but also, on creating an environment where women and minority communities could actively participate in the socio-economic and political life of the state.

Administrative Reforms and Good Governance

Recognising the importance of efficient and transparent governance, Karpoori Thakur's second term saw significant administrative reforms. These measures were aimed at streamlining government processes, reducing bureaucratic red tape and promoting accountability at all levels.

Thakur's emphasis on good governance included the use of technology to improve service delivery, implementation of anti-corruption measures and the establishment of citizen-centric initiatives. The goal was to create a sensitive and accountable government that would effectively address the needs and concerns of the people.

In conclusion, Karpoori Thakur's second term as the chief minister of Bihar was marked by the continuation and extension of the transformative policies that had defined his first term. His unwavering commitment to social justice, economic development and good governance left an indelible mark on the state. The achievements and initiatives taken during his term period not only strengthened Thakur's legacy, but also, contributed significantly to the progress and development of Bihar. Thakur's leadership, full of foresight, empathy and a deep commitment to the welfare of the people, remains an inspiration for the coming generations.

❑

The Leadership Style of Karpoori Thakur

As chief minister of Bihar, Karpoori Thakur's tenure was marked by a series of challenges that tested not only his administrative skills, but also, the flexibility of his leadership style. Thakur took over as chief minister during a period of significant political ups and downs. The outcome of the Emergency laid the foundation of a new era in Indian politics; the Janata Party came to power in 1977. Thakur's rise to the position of chief minister of Bihar reflected the changing political dynamics in the state.

Coalition politics: Making alliances

One of the defining features of the political landscape of that time was the emergence of coalition politics. Thakur, who had a background in socialist movements, was adept at dealing with the complexities of building alliances. His role in the formation of the United Legislative Party (Samyukta Vidhayak Dal) in 1967 was a testament to his ability to form alliances and bring together ideologically diverse parties for a common cause.

However, coalition politics brought challenges with it. Political manipulation was needed to manage competing interests, reconcile diverse ideologies and maintain harmony within the coalition. Thakur's leadership style, characterised by consensus-building and dialogue, became an important asset in sorting out the complexities of coalition governance.

Economic Challenges: Land Reforms and Agricultural Transformation

Bihar, with its agricultural economy, had to face deep (acute) economic challenges. The zamindari system, characterised by land concentration and exploitation was a major obstacle in progress. Inspired by socialist principles, Thakur started the ambitious task of land reforms to remove these economic inequalities.

Abolition of Zamindari System: Social and Economic Impact

The decision to abolish the zamindari system had to face both praise and opposition. Thakur's leadership style became evident in his unwavering commitment to the cause despite the challenges posed by vested interests. The social and economic impact of this move was profound. However, the economic reforms also had to face opposition from those people who had opposed the destruction of centuries-old structures. Thakur's ability to deal with this opposition, communicate the long-term benefits of the reforms and implement them despite challenges, demonstrated his determination and leadership even in the face of adversity.

Reservation Policies: Controversy and Social Equality

Thakur's commitment to social justice found expression in his advocacy for reservation policies. The implementation of reservation for EBC had to face controversy and opposition, especially from those who believed that it could reduce the benefits afforded to socially marginalised groups.

Balancing Act: Equal Opportunity for All

Thakur's leadership style was put to the test because he struck a delicate balance between providing opportunities for the economically deprived sections while addressing concerns about the potential dilution of social justice measures. His ability to communicate the intent behind the policies, defend them in the face of criticism and maintain a balance while maintaining the principles of equality demonstrated the astute approach he brought to governance.

Internal Political Challenges: Alliance Tensions

The political scenario in Bihar during Thakur's tenure as chief minister was not devoid of internal challenges. Managing a coalition government requires efficient leadership to ensure stability and efficiency of the administration.

Intra-party Dynamism

The alliance of socialist parties, the United Legislative Party, had its own intra-party dynamics and power struggles. Thakur's leadership style played an important role in maintaining unity within the coalition, addressing internal conflicts and ensuring that the government could govern effectively despite ideological differences.

Economic Policies and Criticisms

Thakur's economic policies, especially land reforms, had to face criticism from various quarters. The challenge was not only to implement these policies, but also, to convince the public and political stakeholders of their long-term benefits. Thakur's leadership style, characterised by transparency and communication, became an important tool in managing dissent and building consensus.

Cultural and Social Challenges

The controversy surrounding the implementation of reservation for EBCs had cultural and social implications. Thakur's leadership style was tested as he faced these complexities while staying true to the principles of social justice.

Social Implications of Reservation

The EBC controversy highlighted the complex relationship between policy decisions and social mobility. Thakur's leadership was helpful in fostering dialogue, addressing concerns and ensuring that the social implications of the policy were considered in the decision-making process.

Administrative Challenges: Implementing the 20-point Programme

Thakur's tenure as chief minister was marked by the ambitious implementation of a 20-point socio-economic programme. This comprehensive policy initiative covered a wide range of sectors from land reforms to employment generation, cducation and healthcare.

Administrative Ability

Implementing such a multi-dimensional programme requires administrative ability and strategic planning. Thakur's leadership style emphasised effective governance and his ability to streamline administrative processes ensured the successful implementation of the programme. The focus on results and tangible impact set apart his approach to governance.

Crisis Management: Dealing with Opposition and Criticism

Thakur's leadership style had to face its toughest test in moments of crisis, especially when faced with opposition and criticism. The controversies surrounding the EBC reservation policy and criticism of economic reforms required a leader who would be able to deal with turbulent situations.

Communication and Dialogue

Thakur's response to opposition and criticism was characterised by a commitment to open communication and dialogue. His speeches and public addresses at such times not only reflect his political acumen, but also, his ability to connect with the public and explain the logic behind his decisions.

Resilience in Facing Challenges

The ability to weather storms and maintain composure in adverse circumstances is the hallmark of effective leadership. Thakur's resilience in times of crisis, be it political opposition or public unrest, reflects his unwavering commitment to his principles and his resilience in the pursuit of social justice.

Lessons from Leadership: Lasting Principles

Thakur's leadership style, shaped by socialist ideals and a commitment to social justice, provides lasting lessons for leaders in diverse settings. Some key principles emerge from his approach to governance and crisis management—

1. **Inclusive Leadership:** Thakur's leadership was naturally inclusive and tried to bring together diverse ideologies and represent the interests of all sections of society. The coalition politics of that time required a leader who was capable of building consensus and promoting cooperation; and Thakur's inclusive approach became a model for effective governance.
2. **Communication as a tool for governance:** Thakur's emphasis on communication, especially in times of crisis, underlines the importance of transparent and effective communication in governance. His ability to explain the reasoning behind policy decisions, address concerns and maintain public trust through dialogue, remains a valuable lesson in leadership.
3. **Commitment to principles amidst opposition:** Thakur's leadership style was characterised by a firm commitment to his principles, even in the face of strong opposition. Leaders often have to face situations where adherence to principles is tested and Thakur's unwavering commitment to social justice principles provides a guiding light for those dealing with ethical dilemmas.
4. **Nuanced approach to social justice:** The controversy surrounding the EBC reservation policy highlighted the need for a nuanced approach to social justice. Thakur's ability to balance the interests of different sections of society, address concerns about policy dilution and maintain a commitment to equitable (just/fair) opportunities exemplifies the complexity of implementing social justice measures.

Legacy of leadership: Beyond challenges

Karpoori Thakur's leadership style, tested on the touchstone of Bihar's political scenario, left an indelible mark on the broader discussion on state governance and social justice. His legacy extends far beyond the challenges he faced and offers a template for leaders navigating the complexities of coalition politics, economic reforms and social justice initiatives.

The enduring respect and admiration that Thakur enjoys even years after his tenure as chief minister, reflects the lasting impact of his leadership style. The title 'Jannayak' is not merely symbolic; this reflects the genuine relationship he built with the people through his principled leadership.

Thakur's leadership style continues to shape the narrative of Bihar's political landscape. The principles of social justice, inclusive governance and resilience in the face of challenges are embedded in the collective memory of the political consciousness of the state. Future leaders often find themselves measured on the scale set by the 'Jannayak' of Bihar.

Economic Reforms: Impact of Karpoori on the Development of Bihar

Karpoori Thakur's tenure as chief minister of Bihar was a transitional period for the economic landscape of the state. From agricultural reforms to employment generation and economic empowerment, Thakur's vision was aimed at creating a more equitable and prosperous Bihar.

Breaking the Chains of Feudalism

One of the cornerstone economic reforms championed by Thakur was the abolition of the zamindari system. This feudal land-ownership structure, characterised by the concentration of land in the hands of a few, had perpetuated economic inequalities and exploitation.

Socio-economic Revolution

Thakur's commitment to social justice found expression in the bold decision to abolish the zamindari system. The implementation of land reforms was a socio-economic revolution, aimed at redistributing land to the landless and creating a more equitable agrarian structure.

The economic impact of the land reforms was two-fold: firstly, it provided economic help to historically marginalised people and empowered them with the means to generate livelihood and secondly, it promoted a departure from centuries-old economic structures, breaking the chains of feudal dominance and economic freedom.

Empowering the Marginalised

Thakur's government was actively engaged in the redistribution of land, while ensuring that it reached those who had historically been denied access to this important economic resource. Its impact was felt not only at the individual level, but also, in the creation of a more egalitarian rural society.

Stimulating Economic Growth

Recognising the intrinsic link between employment generation and economic development, Thakur's policies prioritised initiatives aimed at creating jobs and livelihood opportunities.

Rural Employment Schemes

Thakur's government implemented rural employment schemes to solve the problem of unemployment and underemployment in rural areas. These schemes focused on infrastructure development and emphasised on projects that could absorb a significant labour force. Strategic investment in rural infrastructure not only generated employment, but also, contributed to the overall development of rural Bihar.

Economic Empowerment through Self-employment

Thakur's vision went beyond traditional employment schemes. He stressed the importance of self-employment as a means of economic empowerment. Initiatives supporting entrepreneurship, small-scale industries and agricultural enterprises were launched to create a culture of self-reliance and economic autonomy.

Thakur recognised education as a powerful catalyst for economic progress. His economic reforms included a focus on improving the education infrastructure in Bihar, with the understanding that an educated population was essential for sustained economic growth.

As part of the economic reforms, Thakur's government gave priority to primary education. Investments were made to enhance the quality of primary education with a focus on building a strong educational base for the youth of the state. This strategic move was aimed at preparing a workforce for the challenges and opportunities of the rapidly growing economy.

Thakur's emphasis on reducing school dropout rates was integral to his vision of an economically vibrant Bihar. By implementing measures to retain children in school and reduce dropout rates, he ensured the creation of a skilled and educated workforce capable of contributing to the economic growth of the state.

Economic Policies and Challenges

Thakur's economic policies had to face challenges and criticisms reflecting the complexities of implementing transformational reforms. The abolition of the zamindari system, although appreciated for its socio-economic impact, had to face opposition from vested interests. Critics argued that it disrupted traditional structures without offering a clear alternative.

Criticisms and Opposition

Economic reforms, especially land redistribution, had to face opposition from those people who opposed the destruction of centuries-old structures. Thakur's leadership style was crucial in overcoming these challenges, communicating the long-term benefits of the reforms and ensuring their successful implementation, despite political and social adversities.

Balancing Social Justice and Economic Development

A major challenge was to strike a balance between the objectives of social justice and promoting economic growth. Thakur's nuanced approach was aimed at eliminating the economic inequalities prevalent in Bihar and ensuring that the benefits of development reached all sections of the society. The economic policies reflected a commitment to inclusive development, in which, the intersecting factors of caste, class and economic status were considered.

Economic Impact: Revolutionary Change

Thakur's economic reforms had a revolutionary impact on the economic scenario of Bihar. This state, once burdened with feudal structures and economic disparities, underwent changes that laid the foundation for future development.

Rise of a New Farmer Class

The abolition of the Zamindari system and land redistribution heralded the rise of a new agricultural class. People who were historically disenfranchised became landowners and contributed to the creation of a more equitable and economically vibrant rural society.

Economic Empowerment at the Grassroots Level

Thakur's emphasis on self-employment and entrepreneurship resonated at the grassroots level. Initiatives promoting small-scale industries and supporting local businesses contributed to economic empowerment at the community level. This economic decentralization laid the foundation for sustainable and inclusive development.

The focus on education as an economic catalyst bore fruit, as Bihar saw an improvement in education indicators. A decrease in school dropout rates, increase in primary education and creation of a skilled workforce prepared the state for long-term economic growth.

Legacy of Economic Reforms: Shaping the Development Path of Bihar

The economic reforms initiated by Thakur left a lasting legacy, which shaped the development path of Bihar for the coming years. The socio-economic changes brought about by the abolition of the Zamindari system, land redistribution as well as employment and education initiatives became the fundamental pillars for the progress of Bihar.

Thakur's economic reforms were not merely policy initiatives; they became a legacy of socio-economic equality. The dismantling of feudal structures, creation of economic opportunities and focus on inclusive growth paved the way for subsequent administrations to give priority to the welfare of all sections of the society.

Thakur's economic policies served as a catalyst for future development initiatives in Bihar. Subsequent governments built on the foundation laid by Thakur, incorporating elements of his economic vision into their policy framework. Land reforms, employment generation and focus on education remained key pillars of Bihar's developmental agenda.

Challenges and Controversies: A Balanced Perspective

While Thakur's economic reforms were praised for their transformative impact, they were not without challenges and controversies. Criticism and opposition reflected the complexities of implementing changes in the deeply entrenched socio-economic structures. However, Thakur's ability to overcome these challenges demonstrated the flexibility of his leadership and commitment to long-term goals. From agricultural reforms to employment generation and educational empowerment, Thakur's vision thus laid the foundation for a more equitable and prosperous Bihar.

❑

Karpoori's Political Strategies

Karpoori Thakur's political journey was marked by clever diplomacy, efficient strategies and a deep understanding of the political landscape. Thakur's ability to navigate the complex web of politics contributed to his legacy as a seasoned politician and 'Jannayak' of Bihar.

Voice of the Proletariat

Thakur's advocacy for the proletariat was not limited to decisions only; it found expression in his speeches, public addresses and interactions with the public. His ability to articulate the struggles of the marginalised people, advocate their issues and rally for their rights established him as a true voice for the people.

Thakur's speeches were powerful tools of activism, resonating with the common man and expressing the aspirations and challenges of the marginalised people. His eloquence was not just a political asset; it was a means of amplifying those voices which often remained unheard.

An important element of Thakur's support was his outreach to the public. He remained directly connected with the people, understood their concerns and ensured that their voices were heard in the corridors of power. Thakur's reach made him a leader who not only spoke for the marginalised, but also talked to them.

Thakur's legacy as the voice of the marginalised people lives on in the collective memory of Bihar. The title of 'Jannayak' was not given lightly; it had been earned through years of unwavering promotion for the rights and welfare of the people.

Thakur's proletariat advocacy left an indelible mark on the political discourse of Bihar. The principles of social justice, economic empowerment and inclusive governance became integral parts of the political narrative of the state. His advocacy shaped the expectations and aspirations of future leaders, thereby influencing the structure of governance in Bihar.

Thakur's advocacy went beyond policy decisions; it involved a holistic approach to empowering the marginalised people. From economic reforms to education and reservation policies, his advocacy was a comprehensive effort to address the systemic challenges faced by marginalised communities.

Early Political Chessboard

Thakur's journey to the corridors of power began against the backdrop of the dynamic political scenario of Bihar. Socialist movements emerged in the 1960s and Thakur, deeply influenced by leaders such as Ram Manohar Lohia, became a prominent figure within the socialist ideology.

The political environment of that time was characterised by the rise of socialist movements advocating social justice, land reforms and empowerment of the marginalised people. Thakur's active participation in these movements shaped his political identity and prepared the basis for his future strategies.

Grassroots Level Engagement

Thakur's entry into mainstream politics was marked by grassroots level engagement. He became the voice of the common man, advocated the interests of the marginalised and vociferously raised the socio-economic challenges faced by the people. This grassroots connection later became the cornerstone of his political strategies, ensuring that he remained connected with the concerns of the public.

Building Alliances for Change

Thakur's entry into coalition politics was a strategic move, which demonstrated his ability to build alliances for a common purpose. The formation of the United Legislative Party in 1967 marked an important chapter in the political history of Bihar and demonstrated Thakur's ability to build alliances.

The United Legislative Party, which included various socialist parties, was a united front against the contemporaneous political system. Thakur's role in bringing together ideologically diverse parties demonstrated his skill in fostering cooperation and creating a formidable political force.

Thakur's experience in coalition governance during the Samyukta Vidhayak Dal era prepared him for the challenges of leading a coalition government later in his career. Navigating the diversity of ideologies and interests within the coalition required political acumen and consensus-building skills, both of which became integral parts of Thakur's political strategies.

Strategies for Governance

Thakur's ascension to the position of chief minister in the year 1977 was an important turning point in his political life. His strategies for improving governance with progressive policies and development reflect a commitment to social justice, economic reform and inclusive growth.

Land Reforms: A Bold Step

The implementation of land reforms including the abolition of the Zamindari system was a bold and transformative step. Thakur's strategy was not only to address economic inequalities, but to demolish centuries-old structures that perpetuated social injustice. This move received both support and opposition, demonstrating the political risks inherent in such transformative policies.

Employment Generation: Strategic Rural Initiative

Thakur's emphasis on employment generation, especially through rural schemes, was a strategic move to address the issue of unemployment and underemployment. The focus on infrastructure development not only created jobs, but also contributed to the overall development of rural Bihar. This strategy is in line with Thakur's vision of empowering marginalised people by providing them economic opportunities.

Facing the Challenges of Alliance

Leading a coalition government comes with its own challenges and Thakur's tenure was no exception to it. The complexities of coalition dynamics required strategic political manoeuvring to ensure stability and effective governance.

The United Legislative Party (Samyukta Vidhayak Dal) faced many challenges within the party and Thakur's role was important in maintaining unity within the alliance. His strategy included addressing internal conflicts, managing power dynamics and ensuring that the government could function cohesively despite ideological differences.

Economic Reforms: Managing Criticism

Thakur's economic reforms, especially the abolition of the Zamindari system, had to face criticism and opposition. Managing these criticisms included a strategic communication approach, where Thakur defended the long-term benefits of the reforms and maintained public support through transparent communication.

The implementation of reservation policies, while important for social justice, requires a delicate balance. Thakur's strategy included elimination of the complexities of caste dynamics, addressing concerns about the potential dilution of social justice measures and ensuring that policies were implemented in a way that the principles of equality were upheld.

Crisis Management: A Flexible Approach

Thakur's political strategies were tested in moments of crisis. Whether faced with opposition, criticism or controversies, his flexible approach demonstrated his ability to weather storms and maintain composure in the face of adversity.

Thakur's communication strategy during times of crisis was remarkable. His speeches and public addresses were not only a means of defending policies, but strategic tools for crisis management. By effectively communicating the reasoning behind his decisions, addressing concerns and maintaining transparency, Thakur faced turbulent disruptions with resilience.

The ability to maintain flexibility despite opposition was the hallmark of Thakur's political strategies. Whether it be the controversy surrounding the EBC reservation policy or criticism of economic reforms, Thakur's strong commitment to his principles and flexibility in pursuing social justice goals defined his leadership style.

Legacy of Political Strategies

Thakur's political strategies left a lasting legacy that shaped the political landscape of Bihar. His commitment to social justice, inclusive governance and strategic economic reforms became the benchmark for future leaders.

Thakur's strategies in coalition politics, governance and crisis management became integral to shaping the political narrative of Bihar. The principles of social justice and inclusive development established by Thakur continued to influence the aspirations and expectations of the people.

The enduring respect and admiration for Thakur's political strategies shows its influence on the leaders who followed him. Future politicians often find themselves held to the standards set by the 'Jannayak' of Bihar and his strategies serve as a guide for effective governance.

❑

Crisis Management: Karpoori Thakur's Leadership in Turbulent Times

As chief minister of Bihar, Karpoori Thakur's tenure was full of turmoil, challenges and crises. One of the most challenging episodes during Thakur's tenure was the controversy surrounding the implementation of reservation for the EBC. This crisis tested Thakur's ability to deal with complex caste dynamics, manage political opposition and uphold the principles of social justice.

Introduction of EBC Reservation

Thakur's government introduced the concept of reservation for EBC with the aim of eliminating economic disparities between different communities; while the intention was to provide opportunities for those who were economically marginalised, the policy had to face significant opposition from various sectors.

Criticisms and Controversies

The EBC reservation policy had to face criticisms and controversies. Some people argued that it could reduce benefits to traditionally marginalised groups, while others accused Thakur of pursuing divisive politics. The controversy brought to the fore the complexities of caste-based politics in Bihar and the challenges of implementing policies with the objective of inclusive development.

Thakur's Approach to Crisis Management: Communication and Consensus

Thakur's response to the EBC reservation controversy demonstrated his crisis management approach. There was a commitment to effective communication and consensus building at the heart of his strategy.

Transparent Communication

While facing criticism and misunderstandings, Thakur adopted a transparent communication strategy. While explaining the rationale behind the EBC reservation policy and emphasising its alignment with the broader principles of social justice, he addressed the public directly. Thakur's speeches during this period were not merely a defence of this policy; they were also a means of connecting with the people and maintaining their trust.

Efforts to Build Consensus

Recognising the need for consensus, Thakur engaged in dialogue with various stakeholders. He held discussions with politicians, community representatives and intellectuals to create a common understanding of the policy objectives. Thakur's ability to bridge divides and achieve consensus in the midst of a crisis reflects his commitment to inclusive governance.

Economic Reforms and Opposition: Addressing Criticisms

Thakur's economic reforms, especially the abolition of the Zamindari system, had to face strong opposition from vested interests. The crisis management strategies deployed during this period highlighted Thakur's resilience and determination to pursue transformative policies.

Opposition from Vested Interests

The abolition of the zamindari system disrupted centuries-old economic structures, challenging the interests of those people who had historically held power. Thakur had to face fierce opposition. Critics argued that the reforms were too radical and would lead to economic instability.

Resilience in the face of Criticism

Thakur's response to the opposition demonstrated his resilience and strong commitment to his principles. He reiterated the long-term benefits of the economic reforms and emphasised on the creation of a more equitable society and economic empowerment for the marginalised. Thakur's ability to withstand criticism without compromising the core objectives of social justice marked his leadership style during turbulent times.

Law and Order Challenges: Balancing Security and Governance

Like many states in India, Bihar was also grappling with challenges of law and order during Thakur's tenure. His crisis management strategies in dealing with public security and issues of governance reflect a delicate balance between maintaining security and upholding democratic values.

Naxalism and Anarchy

Thakur's tenure saw challenges related to Naxalism and anarchy in some regions. The complexities of addressing these issues required a nuanced approach that balanced the need for security with a commitment to democratic governance.

Decisive Action and Rehabilitation

Thakur's crisis management approach included decisive action against elements threatening law and order. Along with this, he emphasised on rehabilitation and development initiatives in the affected areas. Thakur's strategies sought to address the root causes of the unrest while demonstrating a comprehensive understanding of the socio-economic factors that contribute to the challenges of law and order.

Natural Disasters

Being prone to natural calamities, Bihar had to face many disasters during Thakur's chief ministership. His crisis management strategies during floods and other natural disasters demonstrated a compassionate and proactive approach.

Flood Management and Relief

Floods in Bihar were a recurring challenge that required an immediate and effective response. Thakur's crisis management included not only providing relief to the affected, but also, proactive measures for flood management. His administration worked towards building infrastructure that mitigated the effects of flooding, showing a commitment to long-term solutions.

Coordinated Relief Efforts

Thakur stressed on coordinated relief efforts involving various government agencies, non-government organisations and community organisations during natural disasters. This approach reflects the recognition of the importance of collaborative efforts in effectively managing crises.

Shaping the Principles of Crisis Management

Thakur's crisis management strategies left an indelible mark on the principles of governance in Bihar. The legacy of transparent communication, consensus building, resilience in the face of opposition and a comprehensive approach to dealing with challenges became the standard for future administrations.

Strengthening Democratic Values

Thakur's crisis management strategies highlighted his commitment towards upholding democratic values, especially in the face of challenges of law and order. His approach balanced the need for security with the preservation of individual rights, setting a precedent for responsible governance in times of crisis.

Inclusive Governance in Times of Disaster

Thakur's emphasis on coordinated relief efforts during natural disasters underlined the importance of inclusive governance. His administration worked towards ensuring that relief reached all sections of society, irrespective of caste or economic status. This approach became an integral part of the principles of disaster management in Bihar.

Lessons for Cuture Leaders

The lasting impact of Thakur's crisis management strategies serves as a lesson for future leaders. His ability to deal with complex crises with a combination of flexibility, transparent communication and inclusive governance provides valuable insights for leaders facing challenges in a dynamic political landscape.

❑

Reservation: Karpoori's Contribution to Social Equality

The lasting legacy of Karpoori Thakur is his commitment towards social justice, especially through the implementation of reservation policies. The historical context of reservation policies in India lies in addressing problems existing due to centuries-old social hierarchies and providing opportunities for representation and upward mobility to marginalised communities.

Caste-based Discrimination

India's social fabric had been ruined by centuries of caste-based discrimination, where certain communities had been historically marginalised and denied access to education, employment and political representation. The caste system reinforced social inequality, making it imperative for the state to intervene with affirmative action measures.

Constitutional Provisions: Paving the Way for Social Equality

The framers of the Indian Constitution recognised the need for corrective measures for the upliftment of historically deprived groups. Article 15 and Article 16 of the Constitution provided the legal framework for reservation in educational institutions and government jobs that paved the way for social equality and representation for Scheduled Castes (SC), Scheduled Tribes (ST) and other backwards classes (OBCs).

Thakur's Vision: Social Justice and Inclusive Development

Karpoori Thakur's political ideology was deeply rooted in the principles of social justice and equality. His vision for Bihar included eliminating social hierarchy and building a more inclusive society, where every citizen had equal opportunities.

Advocacy for Reservation: A Political Imperative

Thakur's advocacy for reservation policies was not only a political strategy; it was a moral imperative. He recognised the historical injustices faced by marginalised communities and saw reservation as a means of eliminating these inequalities. Thakur's commitment to reservation reflected his larger goal of creating a more just and equitable Bihar.

Inclusive Governance: Extending the Benefits

Thakur's approach to reservation went beyond symbolism. He believed in the transformative power of representation and his aim was to extend the benefits of reservation to the economically deprived sections too. The concept of reservation for EBC launched during his tenure was a testament to Thakur's commitment to inclusive governance.

Implementation of Reservation Policies: A Paradigm Shift

There was a paradigm shift in the implementation of reservation policies during Thakur's tenure as chief minister. His government took bold steps to expand the scope of reservation, ensuring that it reached those who were historically excluded from its benefits.

Reservation for EBC: Expansion of the Spectrum

One of the important contributions of Thakur was the introduction of reservation for EBC. The move was aimed at removing economic disparities between different communities regardless of caste. Thakur's vision was to create a more inclusive framework that considered both social and economic factors.

Expansion of Opportunities in Education

Thakur's government increased reservation in academic institutions, ensuring that students from marginalised communities could get quality education. This move was strategic and aimed to break the cycle of poverty and empower future generations through educational opportunities.

Representation in Government Jobs: Breaking Barriers

Thakur's administration worked towards increasing representation in government jobs for SC, ST and OBC communities. This move not only provided employment opportunities, but also, contributed to the creation of a more diverse and inclusive bureaucracy.

Criticism and Controversy: Dealing with Challenges

Whereas Thakur's vision for reservation was rooted in the principles of social justice, its implementation had to face criticism and controversies. Dealing with these challenges demonstrates Thakur's resilience and his determination to uphold the ideals of equality.

Opposition of Vested Interests

The expansion of reservation had to face opposition from those who were opposed to change. Thakur's government had to face criticism from those sections that saw reservation as a threat to the existing power structures. The opposition reflected vested interests that sought to maintain the status quo.

Balancing Social Justice and Economic criteria

The introduction of EBC reservation had to face criticism related to its economic criteria. Critics argued that focusing on economic backwardness could reduce the benefits to socially marginalised groups. Thakur's challenge was to balance the principles of social justice with eliminating economic inequalities.

Economic Impact of Reservation: Empowering Communities

Thakur's commitment to reservation policies had a profound economic impact on marginalised communities in Bihar. The empowerment resulting from increased representation as well as access to education and employment opportunities created a ripple effect on the socio-economic landscape.

Socio-economic Upliftment

Reservation policies contributed to the socio-economic upliftment of the SC, ST, OBC and EBC communities. Increased representation in educational institutions and government jobs led to better economic prospects for individuals and families.

Building Role Models

The increased representation of marginalised communities in various fields led to the emergence of role models. Thakur's approach to reservation not only provided opportunities, but also paved the way for leaders and achievers from historically disadvantaged backgrounds.

Breaking the Cycle of Poverty

One of the long-term effects of reservation was to break the cycle of poverty. Access to education and employment allowed individuals and communities to transcend traditional socio-economic barriers and contribute to the overall development of Bihar.

Challenges and Lessons Learned: A Balanced Perspective

Thakur's efforts in implementing reservation policies were not without challenges and lessons. The nuanced approach he adopted in addressing criticisms and sorting out complexities provides valuable insight for policy-makers and future leaders.

Balancing Social and Economic Criteria

The challenge of balancing social and economic criteria in reservation policies remains relevant. Thakur's experience highlights the need for a nuanced approach that addresses the concerns of all sections while staying true to the principles of social justice.

Continuous Evaluation and Adaptation

Thakur's legacy calls for constant evaluation and adaptation of reservation policies. The socio-economic landscape is evolving and policies must be dynamic to address the emerging challenges and opportunities for marginalised communities.

Thakur's Legacy: Shaping the Social Landscape of Bihar

The legacy of Thakur's contribution to social equality through reservation policies is deeply embedded in the social fabric of Bihar. His vision for a more inclusive and just society continues to influence governance and policy decisions.

Shaping Political Narratives

Thakur's commitment to social justice and reservation policies has shaped the political narrative in Bihar. Discussions on representation, equality and inclusive development remain an integral part of the state's political landscape.

Empowering Future Leaders

Thakur's legacy serves as a source of inspiration for future leaders. The principles of social justice and the lasting legacy of increased representation, economic empowerment and breaking the cycle of poverty through reservation policies demonstrates the transformative power of inclusive governance.

❑

Educational Strategies of Karpoori Thakur

Karpoori Thakur's tenure as chief minister of Bihar left an indelible mark on the educational landscape of the state. His perspective on the goal of education for all in Bihar has made a lasting impact.

Educational Landscape in Bihar: Challenges and Opportunities

When Thakur took over as chief minister, Bihar was facing significant challenges in the education sector. These challenges ranged from low literacy rate and inadequate infrastructure to inequality in access to education, especially in rural areas.

Low Literacy Rate: A Barrier in Development

Bihar, which historically suffered from socio-economic challenges, was struggling with a low literacy rate that hindered its overall development. Thakur recognised the important role of education in breaking the cycle of poverty and sought to address the systemic issues that contribute to low literacy.

Inequalities in Access: The Urban-rural Divide

The urban-rural divide in the access to quality education was a harsh fact. Whereas the urban areas had a relatively better educational infrastructure, the rural areas lacked schools, qualified teachers and resources. Thakur's policies were aimed at bridging this gap and ensuring that every child, no matter where he or she is, has access to quality education.

Thakur's View: Education as a Means of Empowerment

Thakur's approach to education extended beyond mere literacy; it was rooted in the belief that education could be a powerful means of empowerment. His policies attempted to transform the educational landscape, making it more inclusive, accessible and conducive to the overall development of individuals and communities.

Focus on Primary Education: Building the Foundation

Thakur's emphasis on primary education was strategic. Recognising that the foundational years were important for cognitive development, he sought to strengthen the primary education system. His policies were aimed at ensuring that every child received a solid educational foundation, which would prepare the foundation for future educational pursuits.

Reducing Dropout Rates: Sustainable Education Goals

Addressing the high dropout rate was a key component of Thakur's approach. He understood that merely enrolling children in schools is not enough; efforts should be made to create such environments that encourage continuous educational activities. Thakur's policies included initiatives to retain students in the education system and reduce school dropout rates.

Empowering Women through Education

Thakur's commitment to education extended to empowering women by increasing access to primary education. Recognising the transformative impact of educating women on both personal life and society as a whole, his policies were aimed at eliminating barriers in the education of girls and promoting a conducive environment for their academic development.

Development of the Infrastructure: Addressing the Resource Gap

Thakur's quest for education was not limited to policy formation; it included adequate investment in the development of the infrastructure. Construction of schools, improvement in facilities and ensuring that educational institutions have the necessary resources became integral to his strategy.

Construction of Schools: Expansion of Access

Thakur's government started the construction of new schools, especially in the underprivileged rural areas. This move was aimed at expanding the access of education to remote areas, where the absence of schools was an important barrier in the access of children to education.

Upgradation of the Infrastructure: Quality Teaching Environment

Recognising the importance of a conducive teaching environment, Thakur's policies included the upgradation of the existing educational infrastructure. This included improving classes, providing the necessary facilities and ensuring that the necessary resources were available for effective teaching and learning in schools.

Economic Empowerment through Education: A Holistic Approach

Thakur's approach was holistic, linking economic empowerment with educational activities. His policies were aimed at preparing a skilled and educated workforce that could contribute to the economic development of Bihar and break the chains of poverty.

Vocational Training: Skill Development Initiative

The incorporation of vocational training in the education system was a strategic move by Thakur. His policies were aimed at increasing the employability of students by equipping them with practical skills and creating avenues for self-employment. Thakur saw education not only as a means of acquiring knowledge, but also as the path to economic autonomy.

Small-scale Industries: Linking Education and Entrepreneurship

Thakur's policies were in line with promoting small-scale industries and linking education with entrepreneurship. By promoting the relationship between education and economic activities, his vision was to create a culture of self-reliance and economic independence amidst individuals and communities.

Educational Reforms and Implementation of Policies: A Systematic Change

Thakur's quest for education included not only the formation of visionary policies, but also, the systematic implementation of reforms. His government worked towards bringing about comprehensive changes in the education system in order to adapt it to the aspirations and needs of the people.

Policy Implementation: Changing Vision into Action

The implementation of comprehensive educational reforms requires strategic planning and careful implementation. Thakur's government worked towards implementing the policy vision and ensured that the benefits of the educational initiatives should reach the grassroots level.

Community Involvement: A Collaborative Approach

Thakur's policies recognised the importance of community involvement in the education system. An initiative was taken to include local communities, guardians and teachers in the process of decision-making in matters related to education. This collaborative approach was aimed at creating a sense of ownership and accountability within communities.

Challenges and Controversies

The endeavour for education for all was not without challenges and controversies. Thakur's commitment to systematic change had to face opposition from vested interests and flexibility as well as strategic decisions were required to deal with these complexities.

Opposition from Vested Interests

The educational reforms initiated by Thakur had to face opposition from various quarters. Vested interests that were resistant to change tried to maintain the status quo. Thakur's ability to deal with these challenges while staying true to his viewpoint, demonstrates his unwavering commitment to educational empowerment.

Balancing Regional Disparities

Bihar's diverse geographical landscape presented challenges in ensuring equal access to education. Thakur's policies were aimed at balancing regional disparities and making educational opportunities accessible for children in urban and rural areas. This included targeted investment in the infrastructure and resources of deprived areas.

Impact on Literacy Rate: A Transformative Legacy

Thakur's educational policies had a transformative impact on the literacy rate of Bihar. Concrete efforts for improvement in access to education, quality and inclusivity contributed to an important change in the educational landscape.

Improvement in the Literacy Rate: A Quantitative Impact

Data shows the tangible impact of Thakur's educational policies. During his tenure, a remarkable improvement was seen in Bihar's literacy rate that indicates the success of the initiative launched for increasing educational accessibility and reducing the school dropout rate.

Empowering Marginalised Communities

Thakur's focus on empowering marginalised communities through education contributed in reducing the educational gap. The increase in educational opportunities as well as access to them for SC, ST, OBC and EBC communities became the hallmark of his legacy.

Challenges and Lessons Learned

Thakur's quest for education had to face challenges and the lessons learned in dealing with them present an outline for future educational reforms.

Continuous Reforms: Ensuring Continuity

A commitment to continuity is required for the stability of educational reforms. Thakur's experience highlights the importance of ensuring that policies and initiatives last more than one term, in order to have a lasting impact.

Adopting Changing Dynamics

The educational landscape is dynamic with emerging challenges and opportunities. Thakur's legacy underlines the importance of adapting policy- making to changing dynamics, incorporating innovations and addressing the emerging issues in the education sector.

Thakur's Legacy: Shaping Bihar's Educational Future

The legacy of Karpoori Thakur's educational policies extended beyond his tenure as chief minister. His approach to education has left an indelible mark on the educational future of Bihar, influenced subsequent administrations and shaped the aspirations of the state.

Political Narrative in Education

Thakur's commitment to education has become an integral part of the political narrative of Bihar. Subsequent governments have cited his policies and foresight, demonstrating the lasting impact of his quest for education.

Thakur's legacy serves as a source of inspiration for future generations. His approach to education as a means of empowerment is influencing the aspirations of young minds and shaping the educational discourse in Bihar.

❑

Opponents and Allies: Karpoori's Political Alliances

Karpoori Thakur's political journey was a minute web weaved by the complex alliances and rivalries of the political landscape of Bihar. The alliances formed by him and challenges faced, were not only links in his political career but important markers that shaped the direction of Bihar's politics.

Early political alliances: Preparing the foundation

Thakur's entry into politics was marked by those alliances that laid the foundation of his future political trajectory. His early association shaped his understanding of the complexities of the political landscape of Bihar and influenced the ideological base of his political journey.

The Janata Parivar: Early political affiliation

Thakur found his early political home in the Janata Parivar, which was an alliance of various political parties that came together against the Emergency imposed in the mid-1970s. With leaders such as Jayaprakash Narayan, the Janata Parivar played an important role in opposing the authoritarian governance and provided a platform for Thakur's political initiation.

Socialist Ideals: A Common Base

Thakur's association with the socialist ideals of the Janata Parivar echoed with his own commitment to the principles of social justice and egalitarianism. Coalition became a test where Thakur's political ideology was shaped; the foundation was prepared for his future alliances and his stance on important issues was defined.

Socialist Leader: Forming Alliances in Bihar

As Thakur rose in the political hierarchy of Bihar, his role as a socialist leader became increasingly prominent. The alliances formed by him during this period reflected not only strategic thinking, but also, a commitment to promote socialist principles within the state.

Janata Dal: A Unification of Socialists

The emergence of the Janata Dal in the 1980s added an important chapter in Thakur's political alliances. This party, formed by the fusion of various socialist groups, made efforts to strengthen the socialist political power. Thakur played an important role in this unification by demonstrating his ability to build bridges within the socialist spectrum.

Alliance with Lalu Prasad Yadav: A Political Partnership

One of the decisive alliances in Thakur's political journey was with the charismatic leader, Lalu Prasad Yadav, who later became the chief minister of Bihar. The partnership between Thakur and Lalu demonstrated a shared commitment to social justice and played a significant role in shaping the political landscape of Bihar in the 1990s.

Dynamics of Opposition: Dealing with Adverse Relationships

Thakur's political journey was marked not only by alliances, but also, confrontation with political opponents. A delicate balance was needed to deal with these adverse relationships because Thakur had tried to stress on his principles while engaging with opposition forces.

Confrontation with the Congress Party: Ideological Differences

Thakur's socialist principles frequently brought him into conflict with the Congress party, a party that historically had an influence in Bihar. His conflict with the Congress lied in ideological differences, especially related to issues of social justice, economic policies and governance.

Challenges within the Janata Dal: Internal Strife

The internal dissent within the Janata Dal presented challenges for Thakur's leadership. Different factions within the party, each with its own agenda and power dynamics, tested Thakur's ability to maintain unity and take the party in a unified direction.

Politics of Alliance: Creating and Maintaining a Balance

The age of coalition politics in India presented both challenges and opportunities for Thakur. As a leader of socialist power, he had to deal with the complexities of coalition dynamics and form an alliance with parties sharing common objectives, while managing different interests.

United Front: A National Experiment

Thakur participated in the alliance of non-Congress, non-BJP parties in the formation of the United Front on the national level. The objective of this experiment in coalition politics was to provide an alternative to traditional powers. Thakur's participation in the United Front demonstrated his desire to explore a new political configuration.

The Dynamics of Regional Alliance

In the context of Bihar, Thakur remained engaged in the dynamics of regional alliance. He formed an alliance with those parties that could contribute to the comprehensive aim of social justice and inclusive governance. This regional alliance was helpful in shaping the political landscape of Bihar and providing an alternative to one-party dominance.

Disagreement and Resignation: Breakdown of the Alliance

The latter part of Thakur's political career saw the breakdown of the alliance and internal discontent within the Janata Dal. Along with the complexities of coalition politics, the alliance broke down due to ideological differences, which defined the later chapters of Thakur's political journey.

Resignation from the Post of Chief Minister

After only two years of assuming office, Thakur's resignation from the post of chief minister in 1977 was the result of internal discontent within the Janata Party. The challenges of managing a coalition government and reconciling conflicting interests tested Thakur's ability to keep the coalition together.

Division in the Janata Dal: Ideological Fault Lines

At the end of the 1980s, the division in the Janata Dal exposed the deep-seated ideological flaws within the party. There was a deviation from the mainstream within the party due to Thakur's commitment to socialist principles and his request to prioritise social justice over electoral considerations.

Legacy of Coalition

Thakur's political alliances, those that were formed as well as broken, left a lasting legacy which is responsible for shaping Bihar's political landscape. The impact of their cooperation and conflict is reflected in the political narrative of the state and the trajectories of political leaders who followed.

Socialist Legacy: Lasting Ideals

Thakur's commitment to socialist ideals became the cornerstone of Bihar's political identity. His efforts to unify socialist forces and promote the objective of social justice paved the way for later leaders who carried forward the torch of socialist principles.

Shaping the Janata Parivar: A Lasting Impact

The alliances formed by Thakur within the Janata Parivar had a lasting impact on the political trajectory of the region. The political unit born from the unification of socialist forces continued to shape the politics of Bihar, even after the 'Thakur era'.

Lessons for Future Leaders

Thakur's experiences in political alliances provide valuable lessons for future leaders in dealing with the complex web of coalition politics and ideological differences.

Balancing Principles with Pragmatism

Thakur's political journey demonstrates a delicate balance between principles and pragmatism. Whereas, he remained firm on his commitment to socialist principles, he also recognised the need for pragmatic alliance to achieve comprehensive political goals.

Dealing with Complexities: A Political Skill

Intensive political skills are required for the complexities of coalition politics. Thakur's ability to solve the complex relationships within and outside the Janata Dal demonstrated an astute understanding of the dynamism that defines political alliances.

❑

The Chief Minister of the People: Karpoori Thakur's Popularity

Karpoori Thakur's political legacy in Bihar is inextricably linked to his popularity among the public. His charisma, commitment to social justice, grassroots level governance and policies of economic empowerment collectively shaped his legacy as a leader who was in line with the aspirations of the people.

Charismatic Leader: Karpoori's Connection with the Public

Thakur's charisma was a defining characteristic of his political persona. His ability to connect with the common people transcended the traditional boundaries of politics and made him a beloved person among the public.

A key element in Thakur's popularity was his background. Born in an ordinary farming family in Pitaunjhia village, Thakur's journey reflects the struggle of countless residents of Bihar. This relatability made him the beloved of the people who saw in him, a leader who understood their aspirations and challenges.

Thakur's personal life reflected simplicity and humility. Despite holding the highest political position in Bihar, he adopted a moderate lifestyle. People liked this pragmatic approach which strengthened the belief that he was a leader who was dedicated to serving their interests.

Thakur's unwavering commitment to social justice and the upliftment of the marginalised communities played an important role in garnering widespread support. His advocacy for the underprivileged combined with tangible policy measures established him as the champion of the people.

The implementation of reservation policies under Thakur's leadership was proof of his commitment to social justice. By providing opportunities to historically marginalised communities, he demonstrated genuine concern for the welfare of the underprivileged.

Thakur's vociferous advocacy for the rights and dignity of Dalits and backward classes made him the beloved of these communities. His speeches and actions expressed a sense of immediacy in addressing the historical injustices faced by the marginalised classes of society, in line with their aspirations.

Governance at the Grassroots Level

Thakur's leadership style emphasised on a connection at the grassroots level. As opposed to traditional leaders working within the scope of administrative offices, Thakur was known for being accessible to people, due to which, he became a chief minister who had the image of living among the public.

The establishment of the '*Janata Darbar*', which was a platform for direct dialogue with the citizens, was an unprecedented initiative. This open-door policy allowed people from all walks of life to take their complaints directly to the chief minister. This promoted a sense of inclusivity and accountability in governance.

Thakur's regular journeys to villages reflected his commitment to understand the grassroots reality of rural Bihar. These journeys were not merely opportunities to click photographs; they were real efforts to connect with the challenges faced by the rural population, through which, his image as a leader who was deeply connected at the grassroots level was strengthened.

Thakur's economic policies had been prepared by focusing on inclusive development, the objective of which was the upliftment of all classes of society. His approach attempted to bridge economic disparities and improve the standard of living of common people.

Nurturing the Agrarian Economy

Recognising the significance of agriculture in the economy of Bihar, Thakur started different rural development programmes. The aim of these initiatives was to empower farmers, improve agricultural practices and promote the overall economic welfare of rural communities.

Thakur's emphasis on employment generation was at the centre of his economic policies. The creation of employment opportunities, especially in rural areas, contributed not only in economic development, but also, social stability and poverty eradication.

Thakur's emphasis on education as a means of empowerment made him the beloved of mothers, fathers and the youth. Initiatives taken to improve the educational infrastructure, reduce the school dropout rate and increase the quality of education reflect his commitment towards investment in the future of Bihar.

Thakur's focus on strengthening primary education was a strategic move. By ensuring a strong foundation in the initial years, he prepared the base for a more educated and skilled population and contributed to the long-term development of the state.

Empowering Half the Population

Thakur's advocacy for increasing accessibility to education for women was not only a progressive stance, but also, a reflection of his commitment to gender equality. By empowering women through education, he contributed to the overall socio-economic development of the state.

Thakur's popularity was not untouched by the challenges and complexities of Bihar's political landscape. Controlling opposition forces, managing coalition dynamics and facing internal discontent were all part of the complex landscape of his political journey.

Ideological Conflicts

Thakur's socialist ideology frequently clashed with the political establishment, due to which, opposition forces would raise questions on his policies and style of governance. Along with raising challenges, these ideological clashes also strengthened his image as a fearless leader who challenged the status quo for the welfare of the people.

The intricacies of coalition politics presented challenges in maintaining a unified front. Thakur's ability to balance diverse interests within the Janata Dal demonstrated his political skills. However, he had to face internal discontent too, which affected his popularity.

Thakur's popularity, which lay in his commitment to social justice, governance at the grassroots level and economic empowerment, left an indelible mark on Bihar's political landscape. His lasting impact on the people of Bihar continues to shape the political discourse of the state.

As the 'Chief Minister of the people', Thakur's legacy has become an integral part of the political narrative of Bihar. His popularity is often mentioned by later leaders and his style of governance serves as a standard for connecting with the public.

Grassroots Level Leader

The governance model exemplified by Thakur is marked by reaching out and responding to the needs of the people. It has influenced the later grassroots level leaders in Bihar. His popularity has set a standard for those leaders who truly desire to engage with the citizens who they serve.

The factors contributing to Thakur's popularity provide valuable lessons for future leaders who want to connect with the public and leave a lasting impact on their communities.

His authenticity and humility made him the beloved of the people. Future leaders can draw inspiration from his approach that lays emphasis on staying true to one's roots and maintaining a real relationship with the citizens.

Thakur's style of inclusive governance, which focussed on direct contact with the citizens and marginalised communities, created trust among the people. Recognising the importance of inclusivity in promoting a sense of belonging amidst a diverse population, future leaders can learn from this approach.

His unwavering commitment towards social justice acted as a unifying force. Recognising the transformative power of policies that uplift the entire society, future leaders can draw inspiration from his advocacy for the underprivileged and marginalised people.

❑

Land Reforms and Agricultural Policies: Karpoori's Impact

Karpoori Thakur's tenure as the chief minister of Bihar was marked by a tangible effort to solve agricultural challenges and uplift the lives of farmers. The land reforms and agricultural policies implemented under his leadership were transformative. They reshaped the rural landscape and empowered the marginalised communities.

Bihar's Agricultural Landscape: Challenges and Opportunities

Bihar's agricultural sector had to face multidimensional challenges during Thakur's time, which included unequal distribution of land and low agricultural productivity. Thakur's approach to land reforms and agricultural policies emerged as a response to these challenges, the goal of which was to create a more equitable and sustainable agricultural landscape.

Historical differences in land distribution perpetuated disparities, due to which, a large part of the rural population was marginalised. Thakur recognised the need for concrete land reforms to eliminate these imbalances and empower the landless and marginalised communities.

Low agricultural productivity increased the challenges facing the farmers of Bihar. Thakur's agricultural policies had been prepared not only to eliminate immediate concerns, but also, lay the foundation for a stronger and more sustainable agricultural sector.

Land Reforms: The Path to Equality

Thakur's land reforms were rooted in the principles of social justice and their goal was to ensure a more equitable distribution of land. The objective of these initiatives was to empower the landless and marginalised communities and prepare a base for inclusive agricultural development.

The Bihar Land Reforms Act that was implemented during Thakur's tenure was a historic law that sought to redefine land ownership patterns. This Act banned land holding, stopped the concentration of land in the hands of a few people and facilitated the distribution of surplus land to the landless.

Empowering the Landless

A key aspect of Thakur's land reforms was the distribution of surplus land to the landless. This initiative was aimed at providing a tangible asset to marginalised communities and promoting economic empowerment and social inclusivity.

Thakur's agricultural policies were designed to revive the agricultural sector, increase productivity and improve the socio-economic condition of the farmers. These policies addressed issues ranging from access to irrigation and credit to technological progress in farming practices.

Recognising the important role of irrigation in agricultural productivity, Thakur's government implemented an initiative for improvements in irrigation facilities. This included the construction and maintenance of canals, tanks and wells to ensure a more reliable water supply for farmers.

Economic Empowerment of Farmers

The goal of Thakur's agricultural policies was to ensure that farmers get access to credit facilities. Financial empowerment was seen as a key driver of agricultural development that enables farmers to invest in modern agricultural practices, buy quality seeds and adopt advanced technologies.

Thakur's emphasis on technological progress in agriculture was helpful in modernising agricultural practices. The introduction of new technologies, improved seeds and efficient farming techniques contributed to increased yield and boosted the overall efficiency of the agricultural sector.

The implementation of land reforms and agricultural policies under Thakur's leadership had a profound impact on rural livelihoods. The empowerment of farmers, especially people of the marginalised communities, became the cornerstone of his legacy.

The distribution of surplus land to the landless not only eliminated historical injustices, but also, led to economic empowerment. Land ownership provided a sense of security and stability which helped marginalised communities to be freed from the cycle of poverty.

The focus on irrigation, credit access and technological progress had a direct impact on agricultural productivity.

Farmers experienced an increase in yield, improved crop quality and a more sustainable approach to farming.

Dealing with Controversies

Thakur's land reforms and agricultural policies were not without challenges and criticisms. There was debate and opposition due to the controversial nature of some of these initiatives due to which, Thakur was required to deal with political complexities while staying true to his vision.

The landowners who were to face losses under the land reforms were vocal in their opposition. The resistance to the redistribution of surplus land demonstrates the vested interests resistant towards systemic changes that tested Thakur's resolve in implementing transformative policies.

The implementation of land reforms had to face political opposition from both within Thakur's own party as well as opposition forces. Strategic decisions are required to balance the ideals of social justice with the practical challenges of understanding political landscapes.

Thakur's land reforms and agricultural policies left an indelible impact on the rural landscape of Bihar. The lasting legacy of these initiatives continued to shape the socio-economic fabric of the state in the coming years.

Thakur's land reforms contributed in redefining rural dynamics, promoting social equality and breaking the traditional hierarchy. The empowerment of the marginalised communities through land ownership became the symbol of progress and justice.

The emphasis on irrigation, credit access and technological progress laid the foundation of sustainable agriculture in Bihar. The impact of these policies was seen in the improvement in the living standard of farmers and overall development of the agricultural sector.

By examining the statistics and testimonials from the period of Thakur's land reforms and agricultural policies, a minute understanding of their impact on the rural communities of Bihar is obtained.

Data pertaining to the period before the implementation of land reforms and after land distribution patterns later on, provides a quantitative insight into the transformative impact of Thakur's policies. The decrease in land concentration and increase in landownership among the marginalised communities are the key indicators of success.

The voices of the farmers who directly benefitted from Thakur's initiative provide qualitative evidence of the positive impact on their lives. The testimonials reflect the narrative of economic empowerment among the rural population, increased productivity and a sense of agency.

Lessons for Future Agricultural Policies: A Blueprint of Progress

Thakur's land reforms and agricultural policies provide valuable lessons for future leaders and policy-makers who want to resolve agricultural challenges and promote rural development.

His commitment to social justice served as a guiding principle in preparing agricultural policies. Recognising the transformative power of policies that prioritise marginalised communities, future leaders can draw inspiration from this approach.

The challenges faced by Thakur in implementing land reforms underline the importance of dealing with political complexities. Future leaders can learn from his ability to balance opposition forces while remaining true to the ideals of equitable land distribution.

❑

Disputes and Criticisms: Karpoori Thakur Under Scrutiny

Karpoori Thakur's tenure as the chief minister of Bihar was marked not only by praise for his transformative policies, but also, disputes and criticisms. A subtle understanding of his leadership, which is shaped both by praise as well as opposition, contributes to an overall illustration of his impact on the socio-economic landscape of Bihar.

Ideological Disputes: A Socialist Stance

Due to Thakur's deep commitment to socialist ideals, he often had to face differences with opposing political groups and ideologies. The ideological contentions that he had to face reflected the radical ideological divide that characterised Bihar's political landscape.

Thakur's socialist principles clashed with the more conservative and moderate ideologies prevalent in Bihar. Ideological differences often became the cause of intense political debate. Thakur was firm in his commitment to socialist values.

Thakur's policies and leadership style had to face strong opposition from right wing political forces. The conservative response was especially clear in its criticism of his initiatives of land reforms and social justice, which had been considered radical by some classes of the political spectrum.

Land Reforms Dispute: Resistance to Change

Thakur's ambitious land reforms, although they are celebrated for their transformative potential, had to face significant resistance from landowners and vested interests. The land redistribution dispute became the focus of criticism and protest.

The landlord class, fearful of the possibility of land redistribution, strongly opposed Thakur's land reforms. This resistance rose from a desire to protect long-standing privileges since the reforms challenged the status quo of land ownership in Bihar.

There was internal discontent with regard to the implementation of the land reforms even within Thakur's own political party, the Janata Dal. Strategic decision-making and negotiation skills were required to maintain party unity in order to deal with this political response.

Reservation Policies: Balancing Social Justice

Thakur's commitment to social justice, especially through the implementation of reservation policies, garnered both support and criticism. The reservation policies that were formulated with the objective of the upliftment of the marginalised communities, had to face resistance from those people who considered them a threat to existing power structures.

Critics of Thakur's reservation policies argued that they perpetuated adverse discrimination and created new forms of disparities. The debate surrounding the reservation policies underlined the challenges of achieving social justice in a deeply stratified society.

Thakur's advocacy for the rights of Dalits and backward classes was appreciated by many people. However, it had to face the opposition of those people who saw it as a deviation from the established social order. Balancing the interests of the marginalised communities with the wider social network (fabric) presented a delicate challenge.

Managing Diverse Alliances

Thakur had to face challenges in managing the diverse alliances within the Janata Dal due to the complexities of coalition politics in Bihar. The dynamics of coalition politics brought both opportunities and criticism for Thakur's leadership.

During the period of Thakur's leadership, internal strife was seen within the Janata Dal which was a coalition of diverse political groups. Factionalism and power struggle within the party presented challenges in maintaining unity and a united front.

Thakur's ability to balance the interests of different coalition partners was vital for the stability of his government. Political dialogue (negotiations) and compromises were integral parts of dealing with the intricacies of coalition politics in Bihar.

Economic Reforms: Criticism of the Implementation

Whereas, Thakur's economic reforms were aimed at encouraging growth and development, the implementation of these policies had to face criticisms related to resource constraints and their overall impact on the economic scenario of Bihar.

Bihar's economic challenges, including limited resources, posed obstacles in the effective implementation of Thakur's economic reforms. Criticisms often revolve around the perceived limitations in realising the full potential of these policies.

Thakur's economic policies that were rooted in socialist principles had to face opposition from business interests advocating a market-oriented approach. Ideological conflicts from an economic perspective contributed to the criticism of Thakur's economic reforms.

Janata Darbar and grassroots level governance: Mixed reception

Thakur's innovative approach to governance, exemplified by the Janata Darbar and grassroots level engagement, received both praise and criticism. Whereas, it was celebrated for its inclusiveness, some questioned the practicality and effectiveness of these initiatives.

The 'Janata Darbar', which provided a platform for direct dialogue between the chief minister and the citizens, was appreciated for its reach and accountability. Thakur's commitment to live among the people was appreciated by many.

Critics argued that the practical challenges of implementing such grassroots level initiatives on a large scale outweigh their symbolic importance. Questions were raised about the stability and scalability of these programmes.

Crisis Management: Criticisms During Turbulent Times

In times of crises such as social unrest or political upheaval, Thakur's leadership had to face scrutiny and criticism. Dealing with crises became a litmus test for his ability to deal with turbulent times.

Incidents of political turmoil and internal discontent within the Janata Party tested Thakur's leadership abilities. Critics pointed to these examples as a sign of his lack of control over his party and questioned his ability to manage internal dynamism.

Thakur's response to social turmoil, especially in the context of protest or agitation, faced criticism regarding the perceived adequacy and effectiveness of the measures taken to address the underlying issues.

Thoughts on Thakur's leadership

The diverse views on Thakur's leadership reflect the complexities of his political journey. Supporters see him as a champion of social justice and a transformative leader, while critics highlight the controversies and challenges that emerged during his tenure.

Controversies related to Thakur's leadership continue to be mentioned in the political discourse of Bihar. His legacy has been shaped by both praise and criticism and remains a subject of analysis and interpretation.

Through controversies and criticisms, Thakur's journey provides future leaders with valuable lessons to understand the complexities of political leadership.

Thakur's resilience in maintaining socialist ideals despite facing ideological conflict and criticism, serves as a lesson to stay true to one's principles despite opposition.

Practical governance: Dealing with complexities

The challenges that Thakur had to face in coalition politics and economic reforms highlight the importance of practical governance. Dealing with political complexities and balancing diverse interests is an integral part of effective leadership.

The initiatives of 'Janata Darbar' and grassroots level governance underline the importance of balancing symbolic gestures with practical considerations. Inclusive governance requires a nuanced approach, which addresses both outreach and effectiveness.

Battles Fought: Karpoori's Political Challenges

Karpoori Thakur's political journey was marked by many battles within his party and on the broader political platform of Bihar. From internal factionalism and coalition politics to external opposition and crisis management, Thakur's battles shaped the political landscape of Bihar.

Internal Battles: Factionalism and Party Dynamism

Thakur's leadership within the Janata Dal was not untouched by internal fighting and factionalism. The complexities of managing a diverse political party posed significant challenges to his rule.

An internal power struggle was seen in the Janata Dal which was composed of diverse political factions. Thakur's leadership had to face challenges from within, including factional competition for dominance and influencing the party's dynamics.

The tug of war for leadership and power struggles within the Janata Dal tested Thakur's ability to manage dissent. Astute political skills are required to deal with internal fighting while maintaining the unity of the party.

Challenges of Coalition Governance

Thakur's tenure as chief minister came during an era of coalition politics, which brought both opportunities and challenges. The intricacies of managing diverse alliance partners added layers of complexity to governance.

The Janata Dal, which had diverse political ideologies, required Thakur to balance the interests of its allies. The delicate diplomacy of managing different political agendas was a constant challenge.

The coalition government had to negotiate between policy differences, especially economic and social ideologies. Thakur's ability to find common ground while advancing his vision for Bihar played an important role in maintaining stability.

Opposition Forces: Challenges from Rival Parties

Thakur's leadership had to face opposition not only from within his party, but also from rival political forces. The challenges posed by the opposition parties added an external dimension to the battles fought by him.

The opposition parties opposed Thakur's socialist ideals and the implementation of his transformative policies. Ideological differences promoted political conflict which defined the landscape of political discourse in Bihar.

Struggle for Public Mandate

Thakur's leadership had to face electoral challenges, with rival parties vying for public mandate. The electoral battles tested the popularity of his policies and the public's perception of his rule.

The period of social upheaval and agitations presented significant challenges to Thakur's leadership. Managing these turbulent times required a delicate balance between resolving grievances and maintaining law and order.

Social unrest often arises from deep-rooted grievances related to land, social justice and economic inequalities. Thakur's leadership was tested in addressing these issues through meaningful reforms.

Strategic governance is required to maintain law and order during agitations. Thakur had to balance the need for public consensus with the responsibility of ensuring the safety of citizens.

Limited Fiscal Resources: Impact on Development

Bihar's economic challenges, characterised by limited resources, posed obstacles to the implementation of Thakur's ambitious policies. Creative solutions and strategic priorities were needed to deal with these economic constraints.

Bihar's economic limitations impacted the scale and speed of developmental projects during Thakur's tenure. Thakur had to deal with these obstacles while attempting to achieve meaningful economic reforms.

The challenge of balancing social welfare initiatives with the imperatives of economic development exposed the complexities of governance. Thakur's policies aimed to strike a balance that would benefit both the marginalised people and the economy as a whole.

Political Reaction: Controversy and Criticism

Thakur's leadership was not untouched by political reactions, controversies and criticisms. The battles fought on the political stage are often centred around the implementation of transformative policies and ideological conflict.

The implementation of land reforms had to face intense political and social reaction, especially from the landlord classes. The protection of long-standing privileges became a rallying issue for those opposing Thakur's reforms.

Thakur's advocacy for social justice through reservation policies had to face ideological criticism. The controversy surrounding reservation underlined the challenges of navigating the political landscape while remaining true to principles.

Thakur's leadership was tested in times of crisis, be it political turmoil, internal discontent or agitation. Crisis management became a crucial aspect of his style of governance.

Internal discontent and political turmoil within the Janata Dal forced Thakur to demonstrate strong leadership. His ability to deal with party dissatisfaction and maintain stability in the face of challenges was a testament to his political skills.

In the era of social movements, a careful balance is required between resolving grievances and maintaining law and order. Thakur's approach to crisis management played an important role in shaping his perception of leadership.

Electoral battles defined the political landscape of Bihar during Thakur's tenure. In the search for public mandate, there was a need for strategic campaigns and messaging to secure support for his transformative policies.

Competition with Rival Leaders

Thakur's popularity competition with rival leaders became an integral part of the electoral battle. Public perception of his leadership and policies played a significant role in shaping the electoral outcome.

Thakur's electoral strategies were influenced by the political dynamics of the time. Battles fought at the ballot box require a minute understanding of the voter sentiment and strategic positions.

The political battles fought by Thakur during his tenure as chief minister left a lasting impact on the political discourse of Bihar. The legacy of these battles continues to shape narratives and perspectives on his leadership.

The political battles fought by Thakur contributed to the changing political landscape of Bihar. Contemporary political discussions continue to reference narratives of ideological conflict, electoral strategies and crisis management.

Thakur's political challenges provide valuable lessons to future leaders to deal with the complexities of governance and leadership. Thakur's ability to balance diverse interests within his party and the broader political landscape underlines the importance of strategic leadership. Future leaders can gain insight from his approach to managing internal discontent and coalition dynamics.

❑

The Architect of Change: Karpoori's Policy Innovations

Karpoori Thakur's tenure as chief minister was marked by a series of innovative and transformative policy initiatives. From land reforms to social justice initiatives, educational policies to economic strategies, his visionary approach has left an indelible mark on the political and developmental landscape of Bihar.

Land reforms: Empowering the rural poor

One of the cornerstone policies of Karpoori Thakur's administration was land reforms, which aimed to address the issues of land-ownership, tenancy and redistribution. Thakur's government played an important role in ending the zamindari system. This was a step aimed at empowering landless farmers and ensuring the uniform distribution of land.

To prevent the concentration of land in the hands of a few, Thakur proposed measures to impose limits on land holdings. Recognising the vulnerabilities faced by sharecroppers, Thakur's government introduced tenancy reforms to protect their rights.

Karpoori Thakur was a strong supporter of education as a means of empowerment. Thakur's commitment to social justice extended to the education sector, where he initiated reservation policies to ensure equal access to educational opportunities to marginalised communities.

Recognising the importance of a strong foundation in education, the Thakur government took the initiative to expand primary education. To eliminate economic constraints in education, Thakur's government started scholarships and financial aid programmes.

Social justice Reforms

Karpoori Thakur's commitment to social justice was reflected in several policy measures aimed at the upliftment of marginalised communities. Thakur's government introduced policies for reservation in government jobs to ensure representation from all sections of the society.

Recognising the need for widespread economic empowerment, Thakur's government-initiated programmes to economically uplift the marginalised communities. Thakur's administration took steps to ensure affirmative action in local governance, thereby providing the marginalised communities with the opportunity to participate in decision-making.

Thakur's tenure as chief minister coincided with significant economic challenges and his government offered innovative policies to address these constraints and promote economic development.

Recognising the need for economic diversification, Thakur's government implemented measures to promote industries and sectors beyond agriculture. A key aspect of Thakur's economic vision was investment in infrastructure. An analysis of initiatives in road construction, energy and other critical sectors provide insight into efforts to build a foundation for sustainable economic development.

Dealing with Budgetary Constraints

Thakur had to face financial constraints during his tenure and his government implemented policies to effectively manage resources.

Thakur's commitment to the welfare of the residents of Bihar extended to the healthcare sector. Thakur's government started rural health programmes to expand health services in remote areas. Investing in healthcare infrastructure was a priority of Thakur's administration. Thakur's government launched public health campaigns for disease prevention and to raise awareness about health practices.

Administrative Reforms

The hallmark of Karpoori Thakur's governance was streamlining administrative processes, increasing transparency and improving service delivery. Thakur's government introduced anti-corruption measures to deal with corruption and increase transparency. Thakur's administration worked for decentralisation of governance through panchayati raj institutions.

Ensuring Law and Order

Thakur's government introduced reforms in the police department to address the challenges of law and order.

Karpoori Thakur recognised the importance of the preservation and propagation of the rich cultural heritage of

Bihar. Thakur's government provided support for literature, art and cultural programmes to promote creativity. Recognising the need to preserve the historical treasures of Bihar, the Thakur administration took initiatives for heritage conservation. The government promoted and celebrated local festivals to highlight the diversity of the cultural landscape of Bihar.

Environmental Protection

During the rule of Karpoori Thakur, focus was placed on environmental protection and sustainable development. Thakur's administration initiated recycling programmes to deal with environmental challenges.

Recognising the importance of water conservation, Thakur's government implemented measures to reduce drought and ensure access to clean water. It promoted sustainable farming practices to balance productivity with ecological conservation. Thakur's rule saw efforts to modernise administrative processes through the adoption of technology.

Increase in Efficiency

To increase administrative efficiency, Thakur's government initiated computerisation of government processes. Improving the telecommunications infrastructure was a priority for Thakur's administration. Recognising the importance of digital literacy, Thakur's government launched several programmes to bridge the technological divide.

Quantifying the impact of Thakur's policies on key socio-economic indicators provides information about the tangible results of his rule. The legacy of Thakur's policy innovations can be traced in contemporary policies and governance practices.

❑

Karpoori's Anti-Corruption Initiative

Karpoori Thakur's tenure as chief minister was one of a strong stand point against corruption. His anti-corruption measures, from legal reforms to administrative changes and public awareness campaigns to targeted campaigns, have left an indelible mark on the governance of Bihar.

Context of Corruption in Bihar: Preparing the Stage

Before delving deeper into Thakur's anti-corruption initiatives, it is important to understand the historical context of corruption in Bihar during his tenure.

Corruption in Bihar had deep historical roots, which were linked to political, economic and social structures. An analysis of the historical (empirical) context provides an insight into the complexities of corruption and the challenges faced by Thakur's government in rooting out this deep-seated issue.

Corruption manifested itself in various forms including bribery, embezzlement, nepotism and lack of transparency in government transactions. Public dissatisfaction with corruption was evident and there were high expectations from Thakur to bring about a systemic change.

Karpoori Thakur adopted a comprehensive approach to tackle corruption, which included legal reforms, administrative measures and public-awareness campaigns. Thakur's government introduced legal reforms to strengthen the anti-corruption framework. An analysis of the legislative changes, amendments and new laws sheds light on the commitment to prepare a strong legal infrastructure to tackle corruption.

Thakur's administration established anti-corruption bodies to ensure dedicated efforts in the fight against corruption. This section examines the creation, structure and functions of these bodies, including their role in investigating and prosecuting corruption cases.

Encouraging Transparency

Recognising the importance of whistleblower protection in promoting transparency, Thakur's government introduced measures to protect those who came forward to expose corruption. An analysis of the provisions, effectiveness and challenges of whistleblower protection sheds light on the efforts to encourage accountability.

In addition to legal reforms, Thakur implemented administrative measures to streamline governance processes, reduce bureaucratic hurdles and increase transparency.

Streamlining Procurement Processes

Corruption often finds fertile ground in procurement processes. Thakur's administration introduced measures to streamline procurement as well as reduce bureaucratic delays and opportunities for corruption. An examination of the changes in procurement policies provides information about efforts to increase efficiency and accountability.

Thakur's government established Nagrik Seva Kendra (Citizen Service Centres) to reduce corruption at the grassroots level. Public awareness was an important component of Thakur's anti-corruption strategy.

Thakur's administration prioritised the dissemination of information to educate the public about the harmful effects of corruption. Recognising the role of civil society in the fight against corruption, Thakur's government collaborated with NGOs and community groups.

To ensure a bottom-up approach to tackle corruption, his administration initiated community participation programmes. Thakur's government launched special anti-corruption campaigns to target those specific areas where corruption was particularly prevalent.

Focus on Accountability

Thakur's anti-corruption campaigns often targeted government departments to root out corruption and increase accountability. Public services were the central point of anti-corruption initiatives and action on corrupt practices.

Corruption in public infrastructure projects was a significant challenge and Thakur's administration targeted this area for a special anti-corruption campaign.

Political Resistance: Rivalry and Counter-arguments

Thakur's anti-corruption initiatives had to face political opposition from vested interests. Opposition from within the bureaucracy created challenges in the implementation of anti-corruption measures. The public's high expectations for rapid and transformative changes in the anti-corruption landscape posed challenges for Thakur's government.

In order to assess the impact of Karpoori Thakur's anti-corruption initiatives, a comprehensive evaluation of their outcomes, long-term effects and lasting legacy is required.

Measuring the impact of Thakur's anti-corruption initiatives includes analysing data on the number of corruption cases, convictions and disciplinary actions.

Public perception surveys provide a qualitative evaluation of the impact of anti-corruption efforts on trust in government institutions. The legacy of Thakur's anti-corruption initiatives can be traced in contemporary policies and governance practices.

❑

Last Days and Death of Karpoori Thakur

As the autumn sun dipped below the horizon, it cast a long shadow over the landscape of Bihar. It also marked the beginning of the end of one of the most distinguished political personalities of the state - Karpoori Thakur. The once energetic and dynamic leader who had taken charge of Bihar as chief minister, was now confined to the peaceful corridors of his residence in Patna, battling the ravages of time and poor health.

In these last days, the essence of Karpoori Thakur's life turned into a poignant story of resilience and unwavering commitment to the service of the people. The echo of his political journey passed through the walls of his modest home, where he had spent countless hours strategising, arguing and envisioning a better Bihar.

During this period, Karpoori Thakur's health remained a cause of concern for several months. His once strong body had withered and his trademark white dhoti and kurta were hanging loosely on his emaciated form. The tiredness in his eyes was expressing the stories of battles fought, victories achieved and challenges still to be faced. His family was well aware of his poor health and stood by him with unwavering support and every day was a tragic reminder of the inevitable.

The room where he had spent most of his time was decorated with pictures capturing the milestones of his political career. From the crowded rallies to the quiet moments of contemplation, each frame contains the essence of a man who rose from humble beginnings and became the voice of the people. The walls appeared to be whispering the stories of a leader who had advocated for social justice as well as the interests of the marginalised people and wrote a legacy that will withstand the test of time.

Karpoori Thakur's routine in those last days was a slow version of his previous bustling political life. The once crowded sitting rooms and lively political discussions had been replaced by quiet conversation and occasional meetings with well-wishers. His family would take turns sitting with him, narrate past incidents, laugh and joke and sometimes, embrace the poignant silence that hung in the air.

Despite his physical weakness, the fire of conviction was still burning within Karpoori Thakur. Despite his growing age, his mind continued to remain sharp and coherent. He continued to express concern for the state of Bihar and its people, discussing political developments with those seeking his guidance. His thoughts were a blend of experience and knowledge, which were evidence of a lifetime dedicated to public service.

In the peace of his home, Karpoori Thakur found solace in remembering once again, the ideals that had given impetus to his political journey. He reflected on the struggles of his early years, the movements he launched and the policies he implemented for the welfare of the people. His commitment to social justice, exemplified by the implementation of the reservation policy for economically backward classes, remained the cornerstone of his legacy.

The atmosphere was filled with nostalgia as political leaders, both allies and opponents, came to pay their respects to him. They acknowledged the deep impact he had on the political landscape of Bihar and the indelible mark he left in the hearts of the people. When they talked to him, Karpoori Thakur remained the epitome of humility. He acknowledged the collective effort that had shaped the course of his political career.

The medical team caring for Karpoori Thakur worked diligently to ease his suffering, but the harsh ravages of time took their toll on him. The physical pain was obvious, yet he endured it with a steadfast grace that transcended the limitations of his mortal body. The aura of an experienced leader, undisturbed by the limitations of his physical form, continued to emanate from him.

These evenings were perhaps the most contemplative moments of Karpoori Thakur's last days. As the sun would set, casting a warm glow over the city of Patna, he would often sit near the window and watch the changing colours of the sky. During these moments, his mind appeared to be wandering in the depths of time, remembering the stages of his journey that had lasted for decades.

His family, understanding the depth of these silent thoughts, respected his need for solitude. They watched from afar as he immersed himself in a web of memories—the triumphs, failures, alliances and ideological battles that had defined his political career. It seemed as if he was saying goodbye to each chapter of his life, finding closure in the mosaic of experiences that had shaped him.

Amidst these contemplations, Karpoori Thakur continued to receive messages of support from the people of Bihar. Letters, cards and notes of good wishes started arriving, each of which contained a feeling of gratitude and admiration for the man who had dedicated his life to the service of the state. The outpouring of love is a poignant reminder of the profound impact he had on the lives of countless individuals.

As the days passed, the inevitability of the situation became more and more apparent. The once vivacious leader was now confined to his bed, surrounded by the love and care of his family. His breathing, laboured yet rhythmic, was echoing in the otherwise silent room. The flickering flame of life seemed to be dancing in harmony with the memories shining in the recesses of his consciousness.

It was a calm, moonlit night on 17 February 1988, when Karpoori Thakur took his last breath. With the news of his death, a wave of mourning spread across the entire state of Bihar and outside it because the state had lost a great leader. The tricolour flag was placed on his mortal remains as a symbolic tribute to the man who dedicated his life to the service of the nation.

The last journey that followed was extremely sorrowful, in which, people from all walks of life had gathered to bid farewell to their beloved leader. The streets of Patna were filled with mourners and a collective feeling of loss was visible on their faces. The slogans that had once been raised in support of Karpoori Thakur, now turned into a farewell chorus, which were a tragic acceptance of the end of an era.

However, his legacy was not limited only to the mortal realm. It lived on in the policies that had reshaped the socio-political landscape of Bihar, in the hearts of those people who found voice through his leadership. His last days mark the conclusion of a remarkable journey in Indian political history, but the impact he made, lives on as testament to the enduring strength of principled leadership.

After his death, Bihar was struggling with an emptiness that seemed impossible to overcome. Recognising the need to carry forward the torch of social justice and inclusive governance lit by him, his political contemporaries and successors accepted the challenges ahead. The echo of his ideals continued to reverberate through the corridors of power, serving as a constant reminder of the responsibility that comes with public service.

❑

Karpoori Thakur: Important Milestones

Karpoori Thakur's life journey, marked by his eternal quest for flexibility, dedication and social justice, was full of many milestones which shaped the political scenario of Bihar. Each step in his remarkable journey reflected the commitment to the betterment of the society and left an indelible mark on the hearts of the people.

Humble Beginnings in Pitaunjhia

He was born in Pitaunjhia, a small village in Bihar. His humble origins set the stage for a life dedicated to the upliftment of the underprivileged. Growing up in a family of ordinary means, Thakur imbibed the values of hard work, humility and empathy, which later became the guiding principles of his political career.

Educational Goals and Early Activity

Despite financial constraints, Thakur displayed a sharp intellect and a thirst for knowledge. He developed an interest in social issues during his education. During these early years, he became actively involved in student politics and laid the foundation for a lifelong commitment to public service.

Leadership in the JP movement

With the advent of the JP (Jayaprakash Narayan) movement in the 1970s, a seismogenic change was seen in Indian politics. Karpoori Thakur emerged as a prominent leader in this mass movement advocating the end of corruption, establishment of democracy and promotion of social justice. His role in the movement brought him into the national spotlight, earning him the nickname, 'Jannayak'.

Chief Minister of Bihar – A Historic Moment

Riding the wave of the JP movement, Karpoori Thakur took over as the chief minister of Bihar in 1977. This was a historic moment in his career, as he became the first leader of a backward class to hold this honourable position. His tenure was characterised by courageous and transformative policies whose aim was to uplift the marginalised sections of the society.

Reservation for Economically Backward Classes

One of the defining moments of Thakur's tenure as Chief Minister was the implementation of reservation for economically backward classes. In a groundbreaking move, he expanded the scope of positive action beyond caste considerations and ensured that there was access to opportunity even in dire economic circumstances. The purpose of this unprecedented policy was to create a more just society and it remains the cornerstone of Thakur's legacy.

Thakur's commitment towards the welfare of the poor was further underlined by the beginning of his pro-poor policies. From land reforms to the establishment of schools and hospitals in rural areas, many steps were taken during his tenure to eliminate the socio-economic inequalities prevalent in Bihar. Thakur's administration worked tirelessly to bridge the gap between the privileged and the underprivileged.

Resignation on Moral Grounds

In a rare display of moral fortitude, Karpoori Thakur resigned as Chief Minister in 1979, citing differences within the party and feelings of betrayal by some colleagues. While many people were surprised by this decision, it revealed Thakur's unwavering commitment to principles rather than power. This incident left a lasting impression on the political landscape of Bihar, strengthening his reputation as a leader guided by integrity.

Advocacy of Hindi

Karpoori Thakur was a strong supporter of promoting Hindi as the national language. He believed that the widespread use of Hindi would bridge the linguistic divide and foster a sense of unity among the diverse population of India. His efforts to popularise Hindi as a medium in education and administration reflect his vision of a linguistically unified nation.

Legacy in Education

His commitment to education as a tool of empowerment was manifested in his efforts to expand educational opportunities. Under his leadership, initiatives were started to improve the quality of education in Bihar, especially in rural areas. Schools and colleges were established, laying the foundation for a more literate and enlightened society.

Last Years and Lasting Legacy

As the years passed, Thakur's health began to deteriorate. However, even in his later years, he remained an influential person. He was sought after for his intelligence and insight. His death in 1988 marked the end of an era, but his legacy lives on in the hearts of those people who were influenced by his vision for a fair and just society.

Posthumous Recognition

In view of his immeasurable contribution, various institutions and awards have been named after Karpoori Thakur. They are constant reminders of a man who dedicated his life to the service of the people and the upliftment of the marginalised people.

Summarising these milestones, it becomes clear that Karpoori Thakur's life was not just a chronological progression, but a narrative woven from the threads of compassion, courage and a constant pursuit of justice. His journey, full of triumphs and challenges, serves as an enduring source of inspiration for future generations, reminding them of the transformative power of principled leadership. This chapter that is based on these important milestones, attempts to capture the essence of a man whose life story keeps echoing in the corridors of the political history of Bihar.

❑

True Guardian of Socialism

Karpoori Thakur remained in jail for 26 months during the 'Quit India Movement'. Along with living a simple and straightforward life, he was a dynamic speaker and visionary leader who gained popularity and reached the pinnacle of Bihar's politics. His village Pitaunjhia in Samastipur has now been renamed 'Karpoori Gram (Village)'.

This was the period when money power and strong-arm tactics were used openly in the elections held in Bihar. Karpoori continued to oppose this. He always remained in favour of giving tickets only to candidates with an honest and clean image.

There is an incident from the year 1985. Under the democratic system, the party's parliamentary committee in the Lok Dal had free rein to distribute tickets to its candidates in the elections. Jageshwar Mandal was the chairman of the parliamentary board. The central leadership had put Raj Narayan in charge and sent him to Patna. The parliamentary board had named Karpoori Thakur as the candidate from Samastipur and his son, Ramnath Thakur from Kalyanpur constituency. When Karpoori got wind of this, Raj Narayan had already boarded the plane for Delhi. Karpoori somehow reached the plane and requested Raj Narayan to show him the list of candidates. Seeing his son's name in the list, he became angry and crossed out his name from the list and wrote that he did not want to contest the elections. There was a stir in the party after this incident. Everyone ran to Karpoori and requested him to contest the elections. Everyone said that Ramnath has been in politics for years and been serving the party. He said that he did not want to promote nepotism in politics in any way. Finally, the senior leaders of the party ended the candidature of Ramnath Thakur from Kalyanpur. Only then did he agree to contest the elections and he achieved victory.

Born in a barber family in Bihar, Thakur was a member of the Akhil Bharatiya Chhatra Sangh (All India Students' Federation). Loknayak Jayaprakash Narayan and socialist thinker, Dr. Ram Manohar Lohia, were his political gurus. He had a deep commitment to fundamental modern values like democracy, secularism, civil liberties and human rights. Along with his proud personality, his simplicity and quality of not taking the slightest advantage of his position for the benefit of his family and friends, was also linked to the Gandhian-Socialist stream.

Being a committed socialist, he always tried to bring forward the underprivileged groups, but he considered himself to be the representative of the public of entire Bihar. Many obstacles, including his 'low' caste, kept coming in his way, but he faced them with his political struggle and ideological commitment. He never resorted to communal casteism and casteist identity. Thus, he became famous, not as a leader of a particular caste, but as a 'Jannayak' - people's leader.

Karpoori Thakur was a leader of great versatility. As much as he was involved in politics and socialist ideology, he was equally well versed in literature, art and culture. People in the know say that a bag full of books often accompanied him on every journey. He had his own training in socialist ideology. However, he used to imbibe all the transformative ideas including those of Phule, Ambedkar and Periyar.

During the independence struggle, Karpoori Thakur had written a poem titled '*We have come to stir the nation awake*' –

We have come to stir the nation awake,

Breathe life into the dead.

To throw the gauntlet at the powerful,

Who does not feed the poor.

Do not push us further, Oh tyrant!

Lest we burn it all to the ground.

Or we have come to sacrifice ourselves,

We have come to stir the nation awake.

This poem had once become the song of '*Prabhat pheri* (rounds at dusk)' in the struggle of the socialist movement. This poem also illustrates that Karpoori Thakur was the leader of the underprivileged-exploited groups. Dr. Lohia's thesis that classes disintegrate and turn into classes and classes come together and take the form of castes, directs Karpoori Thakur's understanding of the question of caste and class on a practical level.

Some Inspiring Memoirs

How rich can a chief minister be? You will be left wondering because there is no limit to this. Well, leave this question aside and tell me, how poor can a chief minister be? Chief Minister and poor? You are lost in thought again, right? Can he be so poor that he doesn't have his own car? Leave aside a car, he was not able to build a decent house of his own despite being the chief minister. What's more, he didn't have proper clothes to wear!

The name 'Jannayak' was not given to him just like that. We are speaking of Karpoori Thakur, the synonym of simplicity and the embodiment of principles. The same Karpoori Thakur, who was the Deputy Chief Minister and then, the chief minister twice. He was a teacher, a politician, a freedom fighter and so on, but his real identity was that of 'Jannayak'.

As Prime Minister, when Chaudhary Charan Singh went to his house, he bumped his head at the low door. He said, "Karpoori, make it a little higher." However, Karpoori said, "Until the houses of the poor people of Bihar are not built, what will happen by my house being built?"

Even today, people have tears in their eyes after listening to incidents of his simplicity. Where is such socialism now? Eminent politicians would start crying after knowing about his pitiful condition.

Went Abroad Wearing A Torn Coat

When Karpoori Thakur became an MLA for the first time in 1952, he was selected to be part of a delegation going to Austria in the same year, but he did not have a coat to wear.

When he borrowed a coat from his friend, it was torn. Karpoori wore the same coat and left. There, when Yugoslavia's head, Marshal Tito saw the tattered coat, he gave him a new coat. Today, a man is identified by his clothes.

Taunted for Asking for a Jeep

Karpoori Thakur was famous for his simplicity. Despite being the Chief Minister twice, he used to travel by rickshaw. He could often be seen on the streets of Patna, travelling by a rickshaw, wearing a dirty kurta and slippers. This was the period when R.J.D. supremo Lalu Prasad Yadav had started climbing the stairs of politics. Lalu, who calls himself the disciple of Karpoori Thakur, bought a Willy's second hand jeep when he became an MP for the first time itself and would travel in it.

An occasion came when Karpoori Thakur needed Lalu's jeep. At that time, Karpoori Thakur was the leader of the opposition in the Bihar Assembly and was unwell. One day he had to go to the Legislative Assembly for some important work. Since he did not have any vehicle of his own, he remembered Lalu. He sent a note to Lalu Yadav through one of his close associates in which Karpoori said that if possible, he should drop him to the Assembly in his jeep.

Lalu Yadav wrote on the same paper, "There is no diesel (gas) in my jeep. You were Chief Minister twice. Why don't you buy a car?"

Despite being Chief Minister twice and Deputy Chief Minister once, he did not have his own car. He travelled by rickshaw. According to him, his income was not enough to buy a car and bear petrol expenses. Look at the coincidence, Lalu Yadav who mocked him, later got into legal trouble in the case of disproportionate assets.

Rejected Indira Gandhi's Offer

The year was 1974. Karpoori Thakur's younger son was selected to study medicine. But he fell ill. He was admitted to the Ram Manohar Lohia hospital in Delhi. He had to have a heart surgery. When Indira Gandhi became aware of this, she sent a Rajya Sabha MP and got him admitted in AIIMS. She also visited him herself and offered to send him to America for treatment at government expense.

When Karpoori Thakur came to know, he said, "We will die, but we will not get our son treated at government expense." Later, Jayaprakash Narayan made some arrangements and sent his son to New Zealand for treatment. Karpoori Thakur's entire life was spent in struggle.

Torn Kurta

Jayaprakash Narayan's birthday was being celebrated at Charkha Samiti Bhawan located at Kadam Kuan in Patna. Leaders from all over the country, including former Prime Minister Chandrashekhar and Nanaji Deshmukh had gathered. Chief Minister Karpoori Thakur arrived wearing a torn kurta and broken slippers. A leader remarked, "How much salary should a chief minister get to live decently?"

Everyone started laughing. Chandrashekhar stood up from his seat, pulled his kurta towards the front and said, "Donate to Karpoori's scarf fund." Hundreds of rupees were collected. When he handed it over to Karpoori and said that he should only buy his kurta and dhoti with it, Karpoori said, "I will deposit this in the Chief Minister Relief Fund."

Not Even a House of His Own

Karpoori Thakur was the chief minister twice, but could not even build a decent house of his own. As Prime Minister, Chaudhary Charan Singh once visited his house. The door was so small that it hurt his head. In western-UP style he said, "Karpoori, make it a little higher."

Karpoori said, "Until the houses of the poor people of Bihar are not built, what will happen by my house being built?"

In the 70's, when the government was giving land at cheap rates to MLAs and former MLAs for private residence in Patna, Karpoori Thakur had flatly refused, even on the insistence of the MLAs. One MLA said, "Take the land. If you don't live in it, your children will live in it." Karpoori Thakur said that everyone will live in his village.

After his death, when Hemwati Nandan Bahuguna went to his village, he started crying after seeing his ancestral hut. He was amazed that freedom fighter Karpoori Thakur, who remained an MLA continuously since 1952 and served as Chief Minister twice, did not even build a house for himself anywhere.

Handed Him a Razor

Karpoori Thakur is considered the messiah of the poor. It is said about him that despite getting power, he never misused it. People associated with Karpoori Thakur say that when he was the Chief Minister of the state, one of his brothers-in-law came to him for a job. He asked the Chief Minister to recommend him for a job. Karpoori Thakur became serious after listening to his brother-in-law. He took out fifty rupees from his pocket, gave it to him and told him to go and buy a razor etc. He told him to start his ancestral business.

Karpoori Thakur, known as 'Jannayak', was very conscious of his principles. He also lived an equally moderate (controlled/disciplined) life. He would wake up at 5 o'clock in the morning. Once, when he was the chief minister, he reached Kapil Dev Singh's house for lunch. The socialist leader Shiv Kumar was also present there. He asked Karpoori Thakur for an appointment to meet him. Thakur told him to come at five o'clock in the morning.

Hearing Karpoori Thakur, Shiv Kumar was shocked and asked, "5 o'clock in the morning? Who will I find there? Who will let me enter the Chief Minister's residence?" On this, Thakur told him that he should come.

Describing this incident, Shiv Kumar wrote, "It was very dark at 5 o'clock in the morning in the month of December." The guard asked him his name, address and occupation and sent him into the Chief Minister's residence. When he went inside, he saw that he was not alone. There were many people there.

Picked up Dirty Plate Himself

It was the year 1972. Thakur was the leader of the opposition in the Bihar Legislative Assembly. Lunch was served for Karpoori and his friends on the main table of his room in the Vidhan Sabha building. Karpoori's personal secretary finished eating first and standing up, went towards the basin to wash his hands. He had left his plate on the table itself. When Karpoori finished his food, he picked up his plate with one hand and his secretary's with the other and kept them outside the room. Karpoori also started washing his hands. The basin was a little far away. Meanwhile, the secretary returned. Pranab Chatterjee, who was sitting there, asked him, "Do you know who picked up your plate?"

"Durga must have picked it up," he said. Durga was a staff member of the canteen.

Buxar's former MLA, Pranav said, "No, your plate was picked up by Karpoori himself and kept outside."

'Mukhagni' (funeral pyre) to Dom

This example is enough to understand how revolutionary Karpoori Thakur was by nature. When he was the chief minister in 1977, a sweeper of the municipal council, Thakaita Dom, died in police custody. Thakur held the police responsible for the death. He attended the funeral. Not only this, treating him like a son, he lit his funeral pyre.

Daughter's Wedding

There is an interesting story about his daughter's marriage. The story dates back to the time when Thakur was the chief minister between 1970 and 1971. At that time, he had to go to Ranchi to find a boy for his daughter's marriage. For this, he did not use the Chief Minister's official car and hired a taxi and went to Ranchi.

The marriage was fixed. His daughter was married during his tenure as Chief Minister. His wish was that his daughter's wedding should be conducted in the Deoghar temple with simplicity, but due to his wife's wish, the wedding took place in village Pitaunjhia. Thakur fulfilled his wife's wish, but he had not invited any leader or any of his companions to the wedding. In fact, none of the security guards deployed with the chief minister or any district administration employee were allowed to come.

As Chief Minister, Karpoori Thakur had ordered that no aeroplane would land at Darbhanga and Saharsa airports that day so that no leader could reach there. He got his daughter married with such simplicity.

❑

Becoming a People's Leader: A Political Review

Despite his unique skills and ability to deal with the controversial politics of Bihar, Karpoori Thakur's caste background always influenced his leadership. The questions on which the debate continues, during and after the lifetime of Karpoori Thakur, revolve around his influence in laying the foundation of anti-Congress politics by strengthening the politics of the backward castes of Bihar. He represented the political aspirations of the intermediary castes and posed a tough challenge to upper caste/class politics in the state.

Karpoori was one of the foremost socialist leaders of the state, who gave impetus to the idea of social justice and influenced the political framework of the backward classes. During the 1960s, he emerged as the representative of the political aspirations of the intermediate (backward) castes and thus, posed a serious challenge to political parties like Congress (I), Congress (O) and the Jan Sangh.

Although the unprecedented success of caste-based mobilisation and wider implications in favour of other backward castes became much more noticeable after the 1990s, progress took different trajectories in different parts of the country. In Bihar, some leaders belonging to OBC played an important role in shaping the socio-political form of backward caste politics, which flourished for decades and finally emerged as the ruling politics from the 1990s. Bihar has been a socialist laboratory in its assessment of backward caste politics, where even during the initial phase of Congress dominance, socialist parties had together secured 20 to 25 percent of the votes.

On the socialist side, Karpoori Thakur played a prominent role in the OBC claim and his actions explained the rise of the SSP at the expense of the Congress. Despite adverse circumstances, being influenced by the politics of Ram Manohar Lohia, Thakur emerged as a young and inspiring face of socialist politics in Bihar. Lohia's effective expression of the relationship between the socialist political tradition and the movements of the lower castes helped him recognise the political potential of the horizontal mobilisation of the lower castes on issues of social justice and ritual discrimination and this became the guiding principle of Karpoori's politics.

Thakur's electoral success has been exemplary and he won all the elections he contested since 1952, except the 1984 Lok Sabha elections. His forceful and logical contribution within the Assembly on various issues and concerns of the underprivileged classes of society was matched by his direct engagement with the marginalised people and communities of society and politics. The concept of social justice, the idea of people-centred development and public mobilisation around it were inextricably linked with his thoughts. Those ideas and understanding influenced most of his political actions.

In order to understand Karpoori Thakur's politics, one will have to understand the leadership struggle within the socialist faction in the country. Socialist leaders like Jayaprakash Narayan, Dr. Ram Manohar Lohia, J.B. Kripalani and Ashok Mehta were all great leaders, each supporting his own kind of political freedom and each unwilling to compromise with the other. As a result, with time, all these leaders left the party, defected or were expelled from it. Every time they weakened the party a little by taking their loyal supporters with them.

Most of the Praja Socialist Party (PSP) cadre in Bihar had defected to the Congress in successive waves continuously for a long time — Ashok Mehta left the Praja Socialist Party with his supporters in 1964 and also took an estimated ▯ part of the PSP cadre with him. In a way, the defection in Bihar created more space for the leaders of the backward castes because many upper caste socialist leaders joined the Congress.

In fact, the Bihar State Backward Classes Federation merged with Lohia's Socialist Party in 1957 and then in 1959, after the adoption of the proposal of Lohia's supporters to ensure 60% reservation for OBC, Scheduled Castes and Scheduled Tribes, the entry of religious minorities into organisations and government jobs became the main agenda of socialist politics.

The plan of reservation for backward classes, in a way, widened the gap between the two factions of the socialists—the Samyukta Socialist Party (SSP) and the Praja Socialist Party (PSP). It also alienated a large number of upper caste socialist leaders. The feeling of limited political possibilities was strong among these upper caste leaders, who were later adopted by the Congress party.

The SSP strongly insisted on 60 percent reservation for these groups; the stance of the PSP was soft on this. Moreover, the conflict of personalities and social background among the socialist leaders at the centre had an effect on the deconstruction and restructuring of socialist politics. In contrast to the more grassroots leadership of the SSP, the ruling (elite) class of the PSP was mostly upper caste, educated and largely urbanised.

Due to the social background of the leaders as well as other historical and ideological considerations, the PSP responded only reluctantly to the demand for fixed representation for underprivileged groups (backward castes, tribals and women) in Indian society. This context provided better space and scope for politics championed by leaders like Karpoori Thakur. He became one of the first strong supporters of the slogan '*Sansopa ne bandhi ganth, pichchde Pawan Sau Mere Saath*' (The Samyukta Socialist Party is committed to ensure 60 percent reservation for backward classes) and became the main campaigner for it.

Other popular slogans, such as *'Lohia-Karpoori ki lalkaar, badlo badlo ye sarkar'* (Lohia-Karpoori have given the call for change in political regime) and '*Na sau se kam, na hazaar se zyaada, yehi hai samjwadi vichardhara'* (Neither less than a hundred, nor more than a thousand, this is the socialist ideology), attracted the attention of the backward and Dalit classes of society.

Between 1965 and 1972, Karpoori Thakur, Ramanand Tiwari and Bhola Prasad Singh were the leading forces of the SSP in Bihar but there were differences between them on the questions and issues of the alliance. The wing of which Bhola Prasad Singh was the spokesman, argued for an alliance with the Congress (O) instead of the Congress(R), the Jan Sangh and the Swatantra (Freedom) Party, while the wing led by Ramanand Tiwari supported an alliance with the Congress (R) and PSP. At this time Karpoori Thakur did not have a strong identity in any party.

The general harmony and simultaneous internal rivalry between the two socialist giants, Ramanand Tiwari and Karpoori

Thakur, over the complex issue of the structure of the alliance dominated the political scene during 1969–1971. While a group of the SSP, Congress (O) and the Jan Sangh came together to support Tiwari as a candidate for the post of CM, the other group promoted Thakur's candidature. The apprehension of accepting an upper caste leader as Chief Minister and the risk of an alliance with the right-wing Jan Sangh was considered a betrayal of the interests of the backward classes and socialist ideology. This discussion and the political events that followed were considered to be Karpoori's conspiracy. After becoming aware of the lack of Thakur's acceptability as a leader, Ramanand Tiwari came out openly about the internal disputes of the SSP and wrote vociferously against the Jan Sangh.

In his letter to the chairman of the Parliamentary Board on 28 February 1970, Tiwari underlined that the Jan Sangh intended to push the country towards Hindu fascism. He wrote, 'The fundamental edifice of the Jan Sangh is communal tension and hate. It is unacceptable for the SSP to form a government with the JS. We must always remember that forming a government is only a means, not the end. It seems that we have started considering it as the end.'

The Congress party took advantage of the internal rivalry in the SSP and succeeded in forming a government under the leadership of Daroga Prasad Roy as Chief Minister; however, the government could barely survive for nine months. The irony is that in 1970, Karpoori Thakur formed the government with the support of the Jan Sangh and Ramanand Tiwari became a cabinet minister in his government. In fact, a compromise was reached due to an apprehension about the alliance, identification of the castes of the candidates for the post of Chief Minister, opposition to accept an upper caste leader as CM and a fear of a division in the SSP, which made Karpoori Thakur the Chief Minister of Bihar. The government was a coalition of SSP, Congress (O), Jan Sangh, Swatantra Party and other small parties. Political developments provided an opportunity to the Jan Sangh to participate in governance. This was an opportunity that the party could use to increase its acceptability among voters in the coming years and decades.

Political developments demonstrated Thakur's political art and skills, allowing him to establish himself as the foremost leader of the socialist bloc. Despite allegations of political manoeuvering, Karpoori Thakur emerged as the most accepted leader by various factions of the party.

In most of the controversies at the central and state level, Karpoori Thakur kept himself in the role of mediator and peacemaker rather than the main protagonist and others also chose him. The sequence of events, the behind-the-scenes political strategies and their policy outcomes determined the future of Bihar politics in the coming decades. The policies adopted by Karpoori Thakur after the formation of the government made it clear that the political revival of backward class leaders will continue in the state, at least within the non-Congress structures.

While navigating and negotiating with factionalism within the party, a sense of belonging among the socialist leaders and the various stages of the demands of the popular movements, Karpoori continued in his efforts to create a balance between various factions and emerged as the most acceptable leader in the opposition faction. He used silence, neutrality and obscurity as strategies in the internal strife within the party in the state as well as in national politics.

The day after assuming charge as Chief Minister, Thakur's cabinet took the first major decision to strictly implement the Official Language Act and made the use of Hindi mandatory for all official communications. The newspaper's editorial with the headline, 'Respect for the language of the people, respect for democracy' read, "Chief Minister Karpoori Thakur has informed the press that adverse comments will be mentioned in all their service books."

The previous demands of 'There will be no work in English now, the country will not be enslaved again' and 'The son of the President or the son of a peon; equal education for all, be it *Bhangi* or *Bhabhan*', found its way into the government policy. Earlier, in his capacity as Deputy Chief Minister with the education department, Thakur had removed English as a compulsory subject and made it an optional paper for students in high school.

It was clear to him that students from backward communities and rural backgrounds often failed in the examination because of English as a compulsory subject. Since the students could not pass the matriculation examination, they were not eligible for higher education and hence, they were deprived of employment opportunities. The students who completed their 10th class exams during this phase were often derogatorily referred to as the 'Karpoori Division'.

The upper castes and an influential section of society accused Thakur of bringing anarchy into the education system.

As finance minister, he decided to stop the collection of revenue (land revenue) from the people having 3.5 acres of irrigated land and 7 acres of non-irrigated land. The announcement of the policy was in line with Lohia's slogan – 'If farming is not profitable, there will be no tax on it'. This decision provided much relief to small and marginal farmers. This clearly demonstrated the dynamic socialist character of the government. These progressive announcements eased the apprehension that the right-wing Jan Sangh-backed coalition government would compromise on pro-poor socialist ideologies and agenda.

In 1965, he led a powerful movement against the 'anti-people' and 'anti-student' policies and repressive actions of the Congress government, which gained massive public support. The worried state resorted to violence and the suppression of dissenting voices; the incident of lathi charge on prominent leaders like Thakur and

Ramanand Tiwari became an exceptionally controversial issue for the ruling regime.

Another example of his commitment to people's issues and faith in populist politics was revealed during his protest to ensure job security of employees in industries run by the Tata Company in Jamshedpur. In a show of solidarity with the workers, he began a fast unto death, which continued for 28 days. As a result, the management agreed to minimum wages, weekly holidays and increased job security for workers.

Although the Thakur government (1970–71) was short-lived, backward class politicians tasted success between 1967 and 1972; the SSP made 'backwardness' almost a cult. In the 1967 elections and again, in the 1969 midterm elections, the party became the second largest party. Of the seven chief ministers of Bihar since 1967, four were from backward castes and one was from a scheduled caste.

Although the rise of this form of politics was temporarily halted after the Congress victory in 1972, the socialist strategy of uniting the people was revived during the Jayaprakash Narayan-led movement in 1974. The movement led by Jayaprakash Narayan was the most decisive political movement. After the spread of the 'people's movement' in Bihar, there was a call for 'Sampoorna Kranti (total revolution)' by Jayaprakash Narayan and the subsequent imposition of internal emergency clearly revealed the potential and limits of populist movements in the state/country.

Seen as a challenge and danger to parliamentary democracy and a response to government (outflow?) and corruption, the movement led to violence and repression. The result of the movement, seen and expressed as the manifestation of popular protests, was that 'the people', scorning favouritism and crossing social barriers, united and rose up to challenge the political-economic establishment.

During the 1974 movement, hundreds of trade unions including industrial workers, teachers, engineers, journalists, government and university employees, railway unions, etc. participated in the demonstrations. The main slogan of the rally was '*Poora rashan, poora Kaam, Nahi To Hoga Chakka Jam* (full rations, full work, otherwise there will be traffic jams)'. Echoing the popular sentiment, Thakur appealed to the opposition parties, intellectuals, students and youth to declare 'Jihad' (religious war) to end the 'bad governance of Congress' in Bihar.

Jayaprakash Narayan's appeal and the grassroots level mobilisation of leaders like Thakur influenced the youth and a conference of student representatives from across the state was organised in Patna on 17–18 February 1974. More than five hundred representatives from 135 colleges came to Patna to participate in the conference, where two parallel student bodies - Bihar Pradesh Chhatra Sangharsh Samiti and Bihar Pradesh Chhatra Naujawan Morcha - were formed. The latter represented the students of the Communist Party of India and other left parties, while the former was made up of those who pledged allegiance to the Jan Sangh, Congress (O) and the United Socialist Party.

Events That Took Place During the Movement

On 16 March 1974, five people were killed in police firing in Betia. Over the next weeks, more than twenty-five people were killed in shootings during riots in Munger, Ranchi, Deoghar and elsewhere. Students, yearning for direction and cause, through their organisation, the Chhatra Sangharsh Samiti, were able to convince Jayaprakash Narayan to take over the leadership of the movement. His idea was broad based and he claimed to use this opportunity to shift the framework of policies from political policy to public policy.

Within a few weeks, student and Jan Sangharsh committees were organised in every university and district headquarters of

Bihar. Populism was clearly evident not only in the expression of 'people's struggles', but also, in the broad social base, spontaneous thrust and comprehensive goals of the movements. The fact is that the coming together of two major youth organisations, Samajwadi Yuva Jan Sabha (S.Y.S.) and All India Student Council (ABVP), later SSP and the youth wings of the Jan Sangh, led to confusion about the ideological framework of the movement. In February 1974, C.P.I. separated from this group; after this ABVP, S.Y.S. and T.S.S. formed the Bihar Chhatra Sangharsh Samiti (BCSS), which took a predominantly right-wing stance. These events had an impact on the populist movement.

In the coming years, many conceptual and strategic compromises were made under the pretext of the urgency of the political situation. During Jayaprakash Narayan's movement, ideological confusion was widespread and leaders like Thakur had to face complex questions in their respective constituencies. Although non-Congress politicians had previous experience of alliance with the Jan Sangh (JS), Jayaprakash Narayan's open expression of support for the Jan Sangh was confusing. Speaking in favour of the joint faction of the Janata Party and Jan Sangh in the Parliament, JP thanked the Jan Sangh for the support given to his movement during the Bihar movement. He further said, "If you are fascist, then I am also fascist." In fact, he gave this assurance to the party that he believed that due to the association with the RSS, there was no stigma attached to it. The public statement of inclusion and assimilation of the right-wing political group into the anti-Congress front by the movement's biggest leader, created a complex political scenario for the coming months and years.

However, as the movement progressed and its goals expanded and acquired a specific political character, people also began to ask the question—who would be the harbingers of the 'Sampoorna Kranti'? The confusion, contradictions and complexities of this controversial politics were the biggest challenges for Jayaprakash Narayan, who tried to frame it within the fundamental issues of democracy.

Such complexities and confusions continued to hover in the political landscape and made matters difficult for the Janata Party. There is some room for exploration of the political relations between JP and KT (Karpoori Thakur) in different strategies, approaches and styles.

Nature, character and political restructuring inspired KT to swing between active engagements to background work during the peak phase of the JP movement. Immediately after the imposition of internal emergency in India, he went underground in Nepal and continued his initial organisational efforts from there.

Needless to say, during the JP movement, political idioms, signs, symbols and slogans inspired a section of society that was politically sensitive till now, but remained at the end of political processes. After the victory of the Janata Party in 1977, Karpoori Thakur became the chief minister and he tried to create a political constituency to ensure the stability of the changed political situation in the state. To promote a pro-poor socialist agenda, he introduced a policy to reserve seats in government jobs and educational institutions for backward caste members. It is important to remember that although the Bihar government had listed OBCs in two annexures in 1951 itself, which included 79 castes in Annexure I and 30 castes in Annexure II, the Patna High Court later declared this list unconstitutional in 1964. Reservation in government jobs found its place intermittently in political discussions. However, this did not materialise.

At the end of the 1960s and early 1970s, the continuous insistence and growing political influence of the OBC leaders forced the Congress. The government constituted the Mungeri Lal Commission, in which 128 castes were listed as OBC and 93 castes as MBC. The commission recommended 26 percent reservation in jobs and 24 percent in educational institutions. However, the Congress government did not take any action on these recommendations. It was Karpoori Thakur who had implemented the recommendations of the Mungeri Lal Commission in 1978. As per this policy, provision was made for 12 percent and 8 percent reservation in jobs for the most backward and other backward classes respectively. Additionally, 3 percent of the posts were reserved for women of any category and another 3 percent for those who were 'economically backward'.

The layered reservation policy of the KT government became a significant symbol of success for the backward classes. Finally, the 'backwards' got a small portion of their rightful share in the posts after getting very little representation at the levels of the state bureaucracy, even during the pre-independence period and the British rule. Lohia's vision (expression) of the relationship between the socialist political traditions and the movements of the lower castes were finally realised by recognising 'the political potential of the lower caste horizontal mobilisation on issues of social justice and ritual discrimination'. However, JP was concerned and reluctant about the way in which the reservation policy was implemented by Karpoori and he expressed his disagreement along with his letter of confidence. Political analysts even argued that JP allowed the movement to flourish against reservation.

As a result of this decision, a radical movement against reservation was started by the upper castes and a virtual caste war between 'forward' and 'backward' dominated the political landscape of the state. The interesting thing is that in the protest against reservation for the OBCs, the upper caste flaunted an alliance with the Dalits and expressed it through the slogan, '*Krishi-Harijan Bhai Bhai, yeh pichdi jaati kahan se aayi* (farmers-untouchables are brothers, where did this backward caste come from)?'

In the political spectrum, the upper caste leaders were wary of Thakur's politics and cleverly united the disgruntled MLAs from the ruling and opposition groups. A large number of Scheduled Caste MLAs formed an alliance with the Jan Sangh and led a joint protest in the Bihar Legislative Assembly against Karpoori Thakur. The long-standing enmity of the upper castes with Karpoori Thakur and apprehension about his political efficiency were vindicated by his courageous and controversial decision.

In the absence of adequate political support at the state level, Karpoori Thakur, the pioneer of backward caste politics in Bihar, opted for decentralisation of politics and conducted panchayat elections in 1978. Old officials were ousted on a large scale. They were replaced by a new group of officials who were the loyalists of Karpoori Thakur and his politics, thus gained ground. This signalled the resurrection of backward castes in politics and further influenced and propounded the socio-political discourse in Bihar. The initial shift in the centre of political gravity could be seen at the village level in the panchayat elections of 1978, in the background of the implementation of the recommendations of the Mungeri Lal Commission by the Karpoori Thakur government.

Lohia's prediction that caste-based reservation would lead to deep political changes proved to be accurate. However, a critical assessment of Thakur's preparations reveals that he took bold decisions without strongly uniting the backward classes in the socio-political sphere. Thakur's initial offer of preference incited passions between both the forward castes and Scheduled Castes, who felt threatened by it, leading to its premature demise. Its place was taken by a government dominated by 'forwards and Jan Sanghis'. On Karpoori's political strategies, the Karnataka Chief Minister Devraj Urs said, "Karpoori had entered the ring even before he learned boxing."

❑

Politics of Claim-making Through Assembly Debate

An efficient and effective communication of the political agenda is important for any political party and requires diversified strategies to reach its components. From the early stages of his political career, Karpoori Thakur believed in the power of the mobilisation and collectivity of farmers and labourers against the dominant castes and landlords on the one hand and on the other hand, he used his sharp oratory skills and analytical intervention. His initial efforts of mobilisation through assembly debates was against the landlords, resulting in the liberation of land, which was later distributed among the poor Dalits. Thakur was aware of the rural realities at the grassroots level, as well as initiated in the politics of conflict and he became an inspiring and steadfast leader of the lower-class people. In the post-colonial phase, as a young and vocal socialist leader in the Bihar Assembly, his questions, comments, interventions and overall participation in the Assembly debates are evidence of his wide knowledge, understanding and outspokenness.

Two examples of his intervention in the Bihar Legislative Assembly in February and March 1953 (the second year of his parliamentary career) are relevant here. Speaking on the government motion of the Bihar Public Service System Maintenance (Amendment) Bill, 1953, Thakur underlined the concerns of arbitrariness and abuse of state authority by the ruling party in the newly independent nation-state. Thakur cited the high-handedness of the ruling party (Congress in this case) in the name of maintaining public order. He strongly opposed the government's claim that the Bill has a reformative element and aims to remove the repressive elements of the colonial Custody Act.

While arguing against the proposed Bill, Thakur said that though there was a provision of investigation by the higher judiciary against wrongful custody in the Custody Act, such a measure was weakened in the proposed Bill. To support his argument against the misuse of power by the government, he cited several incidents of the imposition of Section 144, through which the state refused to allow public meetings of opposition leaders and eminent social activists. He accused the ruling political regime of not allowing opposition parties to organise farmers and workers to claim their rights. He further held the government responsible for this, saying that the freedom of the people is being weakened through the proposed law and a referendum is being demanded on the Bill.

While participating in the Assembly debate in support of the motion of a referendum on the Bill by a fellow socialist leader Ramesh Jha on 16 September 1953, KT highlighted the importance of minority opposition voices in protecting the freedom and liberties of the people. Challenging the arrogance of the ruling regime that 'Democracy is the rule of the majority', he quoted political thinker Harold Laski who had said, "The minorities are always the friend of freedom in human society."

Emphasising the need to bring the Bill to seek the opinion of the people through a referendum, he stressed on greater participation of the people in the running of the state and government. His speech explained in detail the disillusionment and lack of enthusiasm in the government as well as fears of a sense of fatalism in the people in the early stages of colonialism. A case had been made to ensure the 'continued cooperation of the voters' in the phase between two general elections. In his detailed speech, Thakur cited several instances of the violation of civil liberties, ban on meetings and rallies by the state and its agencies.

This debate exemplifies Thakur's broad understanding of the criteria and values of democratic politics as well as the various aspects and limitations of representative politics. Through his intervention in the Assembly debate, KT called upon the complexities related to the nature, character, meaning and response of public order vis-a-vis the response of the state. He discussed freedom, equality and the limitations of government affiliation with public opinion.

The deep sense of justice in the context of the parliamentary form of government and electoral politics was examined with a nuanced political commitment. Barely six years after India's independence and within a year of the formation of the first coalition government in Bihar, the state's concern against democracy and the big concerns of the lower-class people were tragically exposed in debates. The debate highlights the tension between the direct and intermediate forms of democracy and explains the ways in which minority/subaltern voices can be weakened in a representative democracy. This points to the dangers of 'democratic ill health', in which citizens were becoming disengaged from the political process and a sense of fatigue and frustration was already setting in among the voters of the new independent nation-states.

In this environment, tools of direct democracy such as referendums, consultation and dialogue can enhance popular participation in the representative system. Underlining his faith in the constant engagement of people with politics and policy-making, KT emphasised that as opposed to representative democracy which was hierarchical, partisan and authoritarian, direct democratic practices like referendums could effectively deal with the issues and concerns of the poor, backward and socially excluded people.

Land Questions, Mobilisation and Challenges for Karpoori Thakur

Responding to the Cut Motion brought by the senior socialist leader Ramanand Tiwari on 20 March 1953, on 'the management of wealth resulting from the abolition of zamindari', Thakur said that only through redistribution of land could the existing inequality and mismanagement be eliminated. He also laid emphasis on establishing the panchayati raj system for revenue collection. In the Assembly debate, he stressed the need to withdraw the collection of rent from farmers by landlords with immediate effect.

On 1 April 1953, speaking once again on the motion of the then Chief Minister on the Bihar Land Reforms Amendment Bill, 1953, KT wanted to set a fixed date for the takeover of the entire zamindari by the state. He said, "If the government wants to make it clear that the zamindari system has ended, then it will have to abolish all zamindaris at once. I am of the view that the postponement is having an adverse impact on the state's interests. Since the discussion of the abolition of zamindari started, lakhs of acres of land became public. Land, dams, water bodies and irrigation channels, cremation grounds etc., have been appropriated, managed and arranged by the landlords in their favour. Whatever is left will soon be taken over by the zamindars too. If the government is really eager to free up spaces for public use, then it needs to act immediately."

Karpoori's strategy gave the impression that he was in a constant battle for position through secret conflict and strove to gain influence and power. In 1977, when Karpoori Thakur became the chief minister, language itself became the subject of politics. His government made it mandatory to do all administrative work in Hindi. Irrigation Minister Sachidanand Singh sent a circular that officials using English in administrative work would be punished and all communication between the central government and the state should be in Hindi and English can be used only after obtaining special permission. On this proposal of 'Remove English', M.G. Ramachandran reacted sharply and, in some ways, it brought to the fore, the role of Hindi as a 'national' language.

Karpoori Thakur himself made it clear that the use of Hindi does not in any way mean abandoning the 'three language formula' and he introduced Tamil as one of the languages to be taught. It is possible to make a separate analysis of the 'Remove English' policy adopted by Karpoori Thakur and it is related to the manner in which the debate over Hindi, before and during the Bihar movement, was conducted. In earlier research on the Bihar movement as part of this project, it had been indicated that leaders such as Phanishwar Nath 'Renu', intellectuals and writers had used local dialects in Hindi to make the written language more popular politically.

Most observers and scholars have drawn attention to the fact that Karpoori Thakur, who was a barber by caste, did not have the essential electoral constituency to counter the increasing political power of the upper backward castes. This may be true, but it also meant that Karpoori Thakur was able to take stands that crossed the limits of demarcated political demands. One such demand that Thakur made was to repeal the Arms Act. He was also a supporter of arming the Dalits, especially in view of the Naxalite movement when landlords were killing Dalits. He was well aware of the fact that the Jagannath Mishra government was giving arms licences to landlords, which led to large-scale killings in Bihar. He was not able to pass a government order that would allow the Dalits to arm themselves. This shows the limits of the populist government and also, that there are such populist measures which no populist leader can incorporate into the process of government. However, it revealed Karpoori Thakur's skill in formulating a populist demand and linked the question of carrying weapons to the social conflict in Bihar.

In his speech in the Bihar Legislative Assembly on 16 September 1955, he said that there was a certain anomaly in the allotment of arms licences to people in Bihar. After this, he made the question of taking up arms a test for democracy. He exposed the hypocrisy of those people who had said that repealing the Arms Act would make the rich more violent towards the poor. He further said that even when the Arms Act was in effect, there had been incidents where rich landlords had killed tenant farmers in Purnea. Then, he said a shocking thing that weapons can be used to organise the tenant farmers and workers. He said, "If this law is repealed, then the poor can also form co-operative societies and village panchayats are also forming them and it is possible that weapons can be purchased collectively. Labour unions can collect money to buy guns and a responsible person can keep the gun in his possession, which will be beneficial for everyone."

Karpoori Thakur's lifespan can be divided into three phases: (a) from his birth in 1921 to 1967 - during this phase, he participated in the Indian national movement for independence, students and farmers agitations and vocalised the common interests of the underprivileged as a prominent socialist leader; (b) from 1967-80, when he was recognised as the leader of the backward classes; and (c) from 1980 to his death in 1988, when he became a helpless leader in search of a new political support base, because a section of the dominant OBC challenged his leadership.

Although this division may shed light on the political career of Karpoori Thakur, there is almost nothing to say about him as the leader of the populist government, no matter how uncertain it may be. Similarly, in the memories of his colleagues, opponents and countless politicians as well as academicians, he stands out as a man who was always in the opposition - uncompromising, honest and idealistic!

As the leader of a populist government, Karpoori Thakur is also the symbol of a specific development within the socialist ideas in India, far from the Marxist tradition. Thakur's tenure in power also points to the first experiments in 'socialist' government and Thakur's importance as the leader of a populist government will perhaps become clearer if we see it in the context of the shift in socialist politics with the advent of liberalisation. Perhaps, Karpoori Thakur's greatest contribution as the head of a socialist government was to point out other possibilities that could be for Lohian socialism and social justice.

❑

Karpoori Thakur: A Timeline

This chapter aims to provide a comprehensive timeline of the life and career of Karpoori Thakur, highlighting the key events that shaped his journey from a small village in Bihar to the office of Chief Minister. The timeline serves as a chronological narrative that allows readers to delve into those important moments that define the legacy of this influential political figure.

1924 : Birth of the great man Karpoori Thakur on 24 January in Pitaunjhia (now Karpoori Gram/Karpoori village).

1932 : Auspicious marriage with Ms. Phuleshwari Devi, daughter of Mr. Moti Lal Thakur, resident of Chandanpatti village of Sakra police station under Muzaffarpur district.

1934 : 9 January. Enrollment in Class 6 in B.M.E. school, Tajpur.

1935 : 15 January. Left school (T.C. No. 34 dated-15.01.1935).

1935 : 16 January. Enrollment in Class 7 at Tirhut Academy, Samastipur (Nomination no.-134, dated-16.01.1935).

1938 : Establishment of 'Youth Association' in Pitaunjhia. Working as a Youth librarian and home village librarian.

1940 : Passed the matriculation examination from Tirhut Academy, Samastipur (Patna University). Enrollment in CM College, Darbhanga.

1942 : Passed I.A. examination from CM College, Darbhanga (Patna University). (Roll Pat No.-1172, Registration _ No.-1627/1940).

Enrollment in BA Part-1. Contribution as a leading soldier of the 'Azaad Dasta (Freedom Brigade)' of youth revolutionaries associated with Lohia-Jayaprakash.

1942 : Active participation in the activities of the student union also.

1942 : Also played an active role in the *Bhoodan* (Gift of land), *Gramdan* (Gift of village) and *Sarvodaya* (upliftment of all) movements.

1942 : Quit studies and actively participated in the 'Quit India Movement' of 1942.

1943 : Contribution as a teacher in Pitaunjhia middle school.

1943 : 23 October. Arrested on charges of revolutionary activities.

1945 : Released from Bhagalpur Central Jail in November.

1946 : Became the General Secretary of the Congress Socialist Party in Darbhanga district.

1947 : Appointed Principal Secretary of Bihar Provincial Kisan Sabha.

1948 : 11 March. Leadership of Hunger March in Sakra (Muzaffarpur).

Elected provincial minister of the 'Socialist Party' formed under the leadership of Acharya Narendra Dev and Jayaprakash Narayan.

1949 : Member of the central committee of the 'Hind Kisan Panchayat', then also as minister. Served twice as a member of the 'Bihar Relief Committee'.

1952 : In the first general elections of independent India held on 26.03.1952, as the Socialist Party candidate from 127 Tajpur assembly constituency, he defeated the great and mighty Congress leader, Mrs. Ram Sukumari Devi by a total of 2,431 votes. This heralded his spectacular entry inside the walls of the Bihar Legislative Assembly.

Tour of West Asian countries and Europe.

1953 : Socialist Party divided. As an active member of the 'Praja Socialist Party' with Acharya Narendra Dev and Jayaprakash Narayan.

1956 : President of the Bihar State Postal Employees Union.

1957 : For the second time, as the PSP candidate from 89 Tajpur assembly constituency in the general elections held on 25.02.1957, he defeated Mr. Nandlal Sharma of the Congress by 10,826 votes. Became Leader of the Legislative Party.

Recognised as the most discussed and popular leader in the Legislative Assembly.

1959 : Re-tour of West Asian countries.

1960 : Chairman of the Bihar State Electricity Board.

1962 : For the third time again, as a PSP candidate from the 101 Tajpur assembly constituency in the general elections held on 19.02.1962, he defeated Mr. Roop

Prasad Rai of the Congress by 18,157 votes and was victorious.

1963 : Chairman of Delimitation Commission.

1966 : 10 August. He became a victim of police lathi charge at the historic Gandhi Maidan in Patna.

1966 : After the unification of the Praja Socialist Party and Socialist Party, he joined the 'United Socialist Party'.

1967 : For the fourth time again, as the United Socialist Party candidate from 97 Tajpur assembly constituency in the elections held on 21.02.1967, he defeated Mr. Bhuvaneshwar Singh of the Congress by 16,462 votes.

1967 : 5 March. Took over as Deputy Chief Minister as well as Finance and Education Minister in the Mahamaya Prasad Sinha cabinet.

As Education minister, he took the bold decision of abolishing English as a compulsory subject in the matriculation examination.

1971 : Relieved from the post of Deputy Chief Minister on 28 January.

1969 : For the fifth time again, as the United Socialist Party candidate from 97 Tajpur assembly constituency in the midterm elections held on 09.02.1969, he defeated Mr. Rajendra Mahato of the Congress by 13,485 votes and was declared victorious.

Elected the national president of the United Socialist Party. George Fernandes was made the General Secretary.

1971 : 22 December. For the first time, he assumed the office of Chief Minister of Bihar.

1971 : 2 June. Removed from power after about five months.

1971 : Remained on a fast unto death in the interests of the labourers in Jamshedpur. His hunger fast ended only after the demands of the labourers were met.

1971 : 20 June. Death of his loving mother, Ram Dulari Devi.

1972 : For the sixth time again, as the SOP candidate from 97 Tajpur assembly constituency in the assembly elections held on 05.03.1972, he defeated the IND candidate, Mr. Kamlesh Rai by 10,568 votes and was declared victorious.

1974 : In order to sharpen the JP movement even more, he resigned from the membership of the Legislative Assembly and became actively involved in JP's 'Sampoorn Kranti' movement.

1975 : 25 June. Declaration of Emergency in the country. Went underground and managed proper conduct of the anti-government movement.

1977 : 30 January. Appeared on the public platform of the general meeting held at Gandhi Maidan, Patna as per decision. Arrested again near Apsara Hotel in Kadam Kuan.

1977 : Recorded his strong presence in the Lok Sabha for the first time as a Janata Party candidate from Samastipur Lok Sabha constituency by defeating Yamuna Prasad Mandal of the Congress (I) by a total of 3,27,434 votes.

1977 : 24 June. He became the Chief Minister of Bihar for the second time.

1977 : 11 October. Announcement of free education till matriculation level on JP's birthday.

Declared victorious for Bihar Legislative Assembly for the seventh time in the elections held on 20th December by defeating Mr. Ram Jaipal Singh Yadav of Congress (I) from Phulparas constituency by 69,000 votes.

1977 : 6,000 unemployed engineers were given appointment letters at Gandhi Maidan in Patna.

1977 : Hindi was declared mandatory in government work.

1978 : Reservation system for backward castes, women and the poor. Under this, 8 percent reservation was made for backward classes, 12 percent for extremely backward classes, 3 percent for women and 3 percent for economically backward upper classes.

1979 : Resigned from the post of Chief Minister on 21.04.1979.

1980 : Mid-term elections in the entire country. For the eighth time in the elections held on 31.05.1980, as JNP (SC) candidate from 95 Samastipur assembly constituency for Bihar Assembly, he defeated Mr. Chandrashekhar Verma of the INC (I) by 27,159 votes and was declared victorious.

1982 : Formation of Lok Dal (A). Made National President.

1984 : Against his wishes, but in the light of orders from the party's central leadership, he stood as a Lok Dal candidate from Samastipur parliamentary constituency. In wake of the sympathy wave of the assassination of Indira Gandhi, the invincible personality was defeated for the first time.

1984 : 18 July. Death of his wife, Mrs. Phuleswari Devi.

1985 : In the elections held on 03.02.1985, for the ninth time, as Lok Dal candidate from 70 Sonvarsha assembly constituency, he defeated the IND candidate Mr. Anwar-ul-Haq by 24,947 votes and was declared victorious.

Played an active and meaningful role as the leader of the opposition party in the Assembly.

1987 : 12 August. He was removed from the post of opposition leader by the Speaker of the Legislative Assembly Mr. Shivchandra Jha, in an undemocratic and undignified manner.

1988 : 17 February. Glorious journey. Under conspiracy or natural death? The mystery continues to date.

After 1988: Various institutions, awards and schemes have been named in honour of Karpoori Thakur in recognition of his contributions in Bihar and India.

2023 : Karpoori Thakur's legacy will continue to inspire political leaders, activists and citizens committed to the ideals of social justice and equality. This timeline serves as a roadmap, guiding readers through the important milestones in Karpoori Thakur's life. From his early years in a small village to the corridors of power in Bihar, each event in this timeline contributes to a rich portrait of a leader whose impact transcends the boundaries of time.

❑